Pra

WILL @epicqwest.c

"Funny, hip, sad, and very, very smart.... This is truly an 'epic quest,' an often hilarious, sometimes heartbreaking search for peace and solace and ordinary human happiness."
—Tim O'Brien

"...Intravenously hilarious."
—Dagoberto Gilb

"...Terrific."
—Denis Johnson

"A brilliant, funny, and ultimately moving book."
—Thom Jones

"At times meditative, at times funny and action-packed, Grimes's prose curves in an arc that traverses the distance from clear to piercing."
—Ann Beattie

"... A remarkably substantial writer."
—Tom McGuane

"Awfully good. Smart. Fast. Sensational, in fact."
—Joy Williams

"Tom Grimes ... calls to mind the writing of many of the bad boys of contemporary American literature—Kurt Vonnegut, Thomas Pynchon, Ishmael Reed and T. C. Boyle."
—Reginal McKnight

"Funny, smart, dreamy ... brilliant, exact and surreal."
—Charles D'Ambrosio

Ludlow Press

Original Fiction

WILL@epicqwest.com

WILL@epicqwest.com

(A Medicated Memoir)

by

Tom Grimes

Ludlow Press
New York
2003

For *individual* copies and info, log on:
LudlowPress.Com
or
write:
Ludlow Press
P.O. Box 2612
New York, NY 10009-9998

To chat with the noble character of this book
log on:
WILL@epicqwest.com

Cover Design by Scott Idleman for Blink! Design

Publisher's Cataloging-in-Publication Data

Grimes, Tom.
WILL@epicqwest.com : (a medicated memoir)
/ Tom Grimes. — 1st American ed. — New York :
Ludlow Press, 2003
p.   cm.
ISBN 0-9713415-7-5
1. United States—college life—Fiction. 2. United
States—social conditions—Fiction. 3. United States—
Information society—Fiction. 4. Epic quest—Fiction.
5.Psychotropic drug satire. I. Title

PS3607.R564 W55 2003
813'.6—dc21   CIP

For
Charles D'Ambrosio
and
as always
Jody
both there through
my dark sunny times

☙

http://Will@epicqwest.com/will/the_memoir_of.htm

Granted, I've been wildly medicated. In

my younger and more vulnerable years just before college, my mother hauled me out of bed where I'd taken to spending most of my time and took me to see a psychopharmacologist.

"What's wrong?" they asked.

"I guess I've kind of lost my faith in things," I said.

Ten seconds later I had a prescription for "The most popular antidepressant in the world." Plus, a little Lithium, to cap any manic phases that might arise.

Other than that, I don't suppose anyone wants to hear about my crappy childhood. All dysfunctional families are alike.

What's important is, I've been on a quest, at least I believe I've been on a quest, to stop the sickness. Information Sickness. People have died from it. They're still dying of it. I am dying of it. We all are.

But there's a cure. And I'm here online to tell you about it.

Welcome to my Web site. Welcome to my memoir. *Hola! Gutentag! Ciao!* Howdy!

Call me Will ... @epicqwest.com.

#

Turbo Gopher Software and Faithful Laptop Companion—
a.k.a. Spunky. Search: will/the_memoir_of/chapter_1
In Which I Wrestle With the Issue of Purpose in an Unheroic
World (and Sense That It's Money)

I was not the embodiment of academic excellence in college. I had trouble adjusting to the notion of homework. In high school we had stopped receiving textbooks when the riverboat gambling resort qualified for non-profit status because it offered a twenty-four hour online chapel in a non-smoking section of the casino. Someone on TV was like, "Our tax base just shriveled." Textbooks vanished.

My first semester's G.P.A. appeared on my transcript directly beneath my mother's credit card number, to which tuition, student fees and sales tax had been charged.

"1.55 is not very good, Will," she told me during a "Friends Talk Free" promotional calling period, then refused to assign any enthusiasm to the fact that my G.P.A. was all prime numbers. "So is 3.55," she reminded me.

We were silent. Ten percent of the charges for our silence went toward my tuition because we belonged to the university's long-distance plan. I broke the impasse by promising to do better.

"Oh, I know. I wasn't lecturing, was I? Your grandparents used to lecture me all the time. I was always like yeah yeah yeah."

I assured her that she hadn't reverted to any platitudes or hollow moral authority.

"God, I hated those clichés. Live within your means. Self-reliance."

"The early bird should take a Xanax," I said.

"Exactly."

In the background, I could hear my mother's forty-three year-old boyfriend, Roger, playing a video game. Mom and "the Rog" met on a discount airline flight between Orlando and Las Vegas. My mother had been a beverage and comfort coordinator, with full HMO coverage and a profit sharing plan, before the airline recorded so many crashes that it was grounded. Roger had upgraded his flight class from coach to business through his credit card Dollars-for-Miles Club, and he and Mom got to talking about the "25 Most Interesting Celebrities" issue of a magazine she'd offered him. After the flight's late arrival, they began dating. Then the airline lost its wings and its stockholders, and Mom went to work thirty-nine hours a week for a talent agency's contracts division. Thirty-nine hours meant the firm didn't have to pay her health or retirement benefits. Her title was full-time temp.

We were silent again. I could hear the rustle of acid-free recycled paper and knew my mother was studying my transcript-slash-billing statement.

"Why are sports and recreation fees higher than your tuition?"

"The school's building a new volleyball center. High tech. State-of-the-art."

"Sand is high tech?"

"It's imported."

We drifted near the end of our conversation.

"It isn't that I'm saying effort is pointless, Will."

"I know."

"It's just that when I see what screenplays sell for today. This morning, a client said, 'Return of the Clone People.' I was like, if they're clones, who cares if they return? You can make new ones!"

"P.S."

"P.S. We had five offers by lunch."

My mother had a secret plan to pitch a high-concept movie. She was convinced that, delivered at the perfect moment, a late Friday afternoon, say, at the end of a particularly profitless week, the stock market closing on a listless note, the Dow Jones average unchanged at dusky winter sunset, a time when all the TV shows had already been converted into movies, every merger approved and consummated, and there appeared a momentary lull in the money machine, some brief, terrifying zone of indifference beyond sequels, at that moment, she believed, an indefinite article could fetch in the mid seven figures. She would simply enter her boss's office, sit down and say, "The…. Coming—Memorial Day."

"I just don't feel I can give you any advice I can honestly say I subscribe to," she told me.

I said, "I understand."

After the call, I left my dorm room. From the campus hillside, I could see the interstate. Its access road's necklace of motel and restaurant signs reminded me of the access road outside of Graceland, where mom and my vanished dad had taken me one Xmas years ago. Just us and a few Japanese tourists walking on a snowy Xmas eve through majestic rooms where Elvis had once worn diapers. The phrase "What golden days!" flashed through my mind. And it suggested to me that I should feel something I didn't, or no longer could.

#

Memoir Therapy, Chapter Two.
In Which I Throw Some Landscape and Personal Existential Quandaries at You

The university I attended was built over a swamp that had been landfilled with garbage and toxic waste, then topped with asphalt. The admissions brochure denied reports of health hazards, calling them "exaggerated." A photograph of students water skiing on the campus's polluted bay, and information on a financial aid package that included tanning salon treatments, promised "successful applicants the best in education and entertainment." The university was able to honor the entertainment part of its pledge as it occupied the buildings of an abandoned outlet mall that had gone bankrupt during the Easter vacation recession when consumer confidence dipped below the critical 230% mark.

We had an excellent food court and cinema facilities, although parking was a problem. Between zones for handicapped parking, multicultural parking, reverse-affirmative action parking, and parking for athletes and their agents, unrestricted parking for ordinary students could be summed up in one hyphenated word: non-existent.

On the bright side, I had been urged and medicated to see, parking fines accounted for 40% of the university's operating budget and were instrumental in financing the new International Volleyball Institute. Administration officials described this as a "win-win situation for everyone."

I was a Virology major. I had decided to study viruses, the ultimate information systems. Viruses are neither living nor dead; they simply copy the DNA codes of healthy cells. Then, before you know it, you're sick, or dying. All because of the transfer of some information.

From the Virology Lab on the top floor of the pre-med building, I could see past the campus dorms and parking fields to the polluted bay. Tall reeds grew along its edge, spreading sleep and headache-inducing allergens as they rustled in the updraft of passing aircraft. Some days, when the sky resembled a scummy gray broth and humidity stalked whatever breathable air was available deep into the filters of the air conditioning generators, everything wavered like a TV image with bad horizontal pull. The concrete, the bookless library, even the dull silver whirring machines marked "Caution: Biohazard."

Across the bay, shacks perched along the water's edge, their window casings tacked over with plastic trash bags. Rusted appliances hunkered in muddy yards and dogs chased children around fishing craft resting on blocks in the dirt driveways. Now and then a trawler moved slowly toward the dying shrimp beds, or circled the oil spill site.

Beyond the shacks lay the airports, one commercial, one military, and a theme park. On foggy, rain-tattered days, airline jets coiled above the campus in holding patterns as fighter planes roared off on practice bomb runs. Petri dishes holding viruses spun on the lab's countertops. Vibrations from the jet's engines made test tubes ping and chink in their racks until I thought I was listening to some bad New Age xylophone solo. I couldn't concentrate unless Walkman headphones blared around my ears. I once wrote that Pb was the periodic table notation for lead.

The only place to escape the bone-thrumming thunder of the jets was in the basement of the bookless library. In the quiet of the shelter, with my medications slowly taking hold and holograms of viruses glowing on Spunky's screen, the absolute certainties expressed in scientific proofs almost convinced me that I was living in a world that made sense.

#

Chapter Three: On Moral Instruction

Determined to make amends for my poor academic efforts, I went to see the student advisor at the University Guidance center, Dr. Mike.

As a student, Dr. Mike had held the intercollegiate golf champion title. Although he never succeeded on the PGA tour, Dr. M. did go on to write a best-selling paperback on the game's virtues entitled, "When Jesus Is Your Caddy." Twenty-five pages, large type. While he studied my academic performance on his large color monitor, I marveled at the fake gold-plated plastic trophies impressively lining his office bookcases. Then he swiveled his chair to face me.

"You bogeyed big time in semester *numero uno*, Will."

I wondered if Dr. M. realized that he'd violated the English-only law in effect on campus. The law prohibited the speaking of foreign languages on university property, despite complaints from the student council arguing that the law infringed on a student's constitutional right to order a burrito.

"Well, we're chucking it. Wiping the slate clean. A fresh eighteen holes. What do you say?"

"You can do that?"

"Will, higher education isn't a hole-in-one. You've got to learn your irons from your woods. You've got to know when to lay up and when to say that par is God's will, too. Our goal is to graduate people, son. Now, how is discouraging you academically going to help? Do you think Jesus went around discouraging people?"

I was afraid to tell him that my knowledge of Jesus was limited to an episode of "Amazing Tales" and videos broadcast by the Christian rock channel.

"Success is a no-brainer. All it takes is following some pretty basic rules. First, you look to me like you're in pretty good shape. So, pick a sport and stick to it. Number two: don't drink to excess on school nights. Three: get involved, give something back. Community spirit, volunteer work, the whole nine yards. Follow? And finally, do you have one of these?"

He flashed a "Safe Sex" brochure in my direction. I sensed by his arched eyebrow that he wanted me to keep quiet and take one. Then he printed out a copy of the schedule he'd designed for me. In addition to Viral Studies, I was enrolled in Great Diseases in History, Existential Philosophy and the Hollywood Tradition,

How To Create An Investment Portfolio, and Advanced Volley-ball. Plus, I sat on the advisory committee to someone running for Student Body President.

"This is a lot of work," I said.

"Son, our job is to train young people. Get 'em up and running. Out into the marketplace."

"My allergies and the jets really affect my concentration."

"Pills. Great new strides in medicine every day."

I wondered if my being on Prozac had turned up in my university dossier.

"Heck, why feel sick if you can just pop a little doo-hickey in your mouth and feel good as new twenty minutes later?" He sprang out of his chair and began to practice his putting along a strip of carpet. "If the noise bothers you, try ear plugs. Buy some study aids. Lay your hands on one of them white noise contraptions. Get creative. Accessorize."

"Why am I in Advanced Volleyball?"

"Wilt, excuse my French, but you don't want to see the sorry-ass crew we'd have to consign to Volleyball 101." He stroked gently, then jerked backwards and cringed when he missed an easy six-footer. "Anyway, you're too young for all this quiet desperation. That's for geezers my age on low-sodium diets and prostate medication. Sports movies, my friend. *Rocky, Hoosiers, Field of Dreams*. Inspiring, mystical stuff. Some god-danged fine performances, too, if you ask me." He pointed his putter at me. "Son, you don't want to overlook the inspirational qualities of great sports films. Plus they're like, what, forty-nine cents for three nights?"

#

Chapter Four: Beauty, Poetry, Love, Death, and Antihis-tamines

During my second semester, I gradually became comfortable amid the Virology lab's electron microscopes. The framed reproductions of viral infection that hung on the laboratory walls began to feel reassuring, and at times I couldn't distinguish them from the "Abstract Expressionist" canvases I had studied in "Art History and Advertising Techniques 101." Hepatitis and Yellow Fever combined static color fields with a teeming sense of linear movement, and I believe the influence of cytomegalovirus can be traced to the vivid cellular-style compositions of Miro and De-Kooning. My term paper would have conclusively established the link between Pollock's "drip painting" technique and cell infiltration patterns in Herpes virus with meningeal involvement, had I written the paper's body and conclusion.

Then, too, I may have adjusted because my new lab partner Naomi was brain-numbingly beautiful, as well as suddenly famous. To me and seventeen million other faithful subscribers of a national men's magazine, the airbrushed image of Naomi reclining in a hayloft wearing only an unbuttoned lab coat and cowboy boots in the magazine's "Girls of Campuses-Near-Interstates" issue captured the wholesome innocence of college life. The poignancy of her vulnerable, in-print admission that, "No, it's *not* true that everybody where I'm from is KKK," moved me as much as any animated Disney adaptation of a classic ever did. Consequently, my love for Na (long A) was pure. I swear I never jerked off to her photo spread, a claim seventeen million other guys probably can't make.

I even wrote her a haiku, with the help of Spunk's "E-Z Poetry" software, on the similar natures of viruses and love:

Lying dormant, you
infect me, parasitic
lover…oooh baby.

Naomi used to tell me that viruses were like men. "First they make you sick," she said. "Then before you're back on your feet, they're off infecting somebody else."

I assumed Naomi spoke from deep experience, as she had seventeen million potential boyfriends. I hated to see her suffer and wished that I could recite classic love poetry to her. But Shakespeare had been relegated to an elective in the Dept. of Sexist-Racist Studies. The only lyric I knew was "Let me compare thee to a summer's day," and the words had been addressed to a beverage juice in a commercial with people surfing.

Naomi wanted to be a veterinarian. What amazed me, and made me want to have children and live in a huge white farmhouse with her, was her incredible sensitivity. I remember how she wept when our virology professor arrived the first morning of lab and demonstrated how to narcotize, mark by perforation of one ear, then "de-life" by cervical dislocation the white mice we used as specimens.

After class, I consoled Naomi, without mentioning that her mascara had run and she looked like a satanist. "Come on, it's not so bad. Look on the bright side. No pain, no gain. Tomorrow's another day. Buy one, get one free."

"I can't stand to see little animals suffer," she cried, still upset about the mouse. "Why do you think I don't eat red meat? Only fish or chicken, sometimes."

I assembled some clichés about the value of stoicism, emotional detachment and all around non-feeling. "Think of how Marsha from 'The Brady Bunch' would have handled it," I said.

Then Naomi's allergies began bothering her and she had a sneezing fit. I gave her an antihistamine, after checking that she wasn't already taking Erythromycin, Ketaconazole or Itraconazole for respiratory or fungal infections, since this combination can cause heart arrythmias. I did consider that Naomi might mistake a heart arrythymia caused by unsafe drug interactions for the pitter-patter of love. But I decided that my love was Platonic, and would remain so as long as I suspected the slightest chance of an emotionally crushing rejection.

"Here," I said, "this'll dry up your sinuses without causing drowsiness. Feel free to operate heavy machinery under its influence."

Naomi took the pill and kissed me by bumping her cheek against my cheek. I was moved. Sharing prescription drugs might be the final romantic gesture. Soon we'd be sending valentines on prescription pads.

But can one expect true love in a world with mood pills and information, information, and more information?

#

Chapter Five: Breakfast, and the Introduction of a Mysterious Character Who Will Figure Mightily in My Quest

The next morning, I found out exactly how lethal information could be.

I had made my way with hundreds of other students to the food court for the most important meal of the day: breakfast. Walking along the campus's wide, open-air promenade, I noted how elegantly it lined up with the runway across the brownish hues of the bay, making it an ideal spot for crash landings. Promotional credit card giveaways and an enlightened "soapbox" speech calling for the summary executions of drivers who failed breathalyzer tests were in progress. Meanwhile, the university's diverse student body congregated in groups according to race, religion, and hairstyle. I saw happy campus bargain-seekers taking advantage of the "fajita special" coupons and pocket editions New Testament being handed out. As jet exhaust, stirred by gentle bay breezes, mingled overhead with fluorocarbons to create a festive blue-gray halo, the pastoral scene almost made me glad my mother had gone into debt for my higher education.

According to a review I'd read in the student paper, the food court had dishes to satisfy every appetite. "For the pastry-craving," it noted, "delectable swirls and contorted shapes of air-blown sugar prove irresistible, with some pastries swelling to the size of stuffed animals. The 'croissant brunch pizza with pseudo bacon strips' perfectly complements a frothy Frappacino, available at the Java Hut, and is ample for two. Hungover carbohydrate seekers need search no further than 'The Trough,' a Formica-topped pasta bar boasting a kitschy '70s look, for heaping portions of boiled starch. The platform shoe cheese shakers rank among the most desirable of collectibles. Don't pocket one, though. Cameras are watching! Those looking to rehydrate after a night of jello shots and shouting at one of the campus mall's sports bars can savor soothing bowls of Vietnamese rice noodle "pho" from the microwave soup carousel, also available with a ginseng booster for stressed, immuno-compromised diners battling the sniffles."

My personal favorite—even though I began to notice that it filled me up but left me hungry—was the fat-free, chili-cheese, egg white soufflé with garlic-mint tortilla chips. It was prepared with a fat substitute patented by the university's new chemical compound specialist, Professor Bones, recipient of the Chair in Viral Studies funded by the theme park and military base across the bay.

And there I was, seated in the food court's Hall of TVs, surrounded by people consuming the same fat-free substitute that had made my low cholesterol soufflé possible, when the university Provost's videotaped address announcing the hiring of Dr. Bones appeared on screen.

"Other than construction of our new parking lot, and work on our International Volleyball Institute," the Provost told university cable access channel cameras, "I can think of no more exciting development for the Campus-by-the-Interstate than the addition of Dr. Bones to our already distinguished faculty. He comes to us after a ground-breaking career at the Dept. of Industrial Agriculture where he single-handedly brought the world into the post-olestra era of low-fat eating."

The being—if he was a being, we had only the Provost's word for it—the being, or entity, responsible for our communally plaque-free arteries and the promise of longer, healthier, more productive lives was suddenly in the vicinity. For some reason, perhaps because of his near celebrity, I sensed that I should feel a kind of gaping, dumbstruck awe, as if my life had suddenly congealed with purpose. I felt a desire to meet, or even just see him. A photograph or video would do, as they had for so many impalpable others.

Instead, the name that had given mankind its first non-biodegradable foodstuff substitute remained ineffable, hovering about the campus like an honorary rumor. Slightly unreal, like my chemically synthetic emotions.

A bit of information containing no discernible meaning.

#

Chapter Six: News, Information Sickness, Paradox, and the Great Indoors

That evening while I was studying, word came during the "In Other News" segment of the telemagazine show I was half-watching that a person on campus had died of what was unofficially called "Information Sickness." An overload of information. A disease so insidious that its spread was relentless, detection nearly impossible, and the infection rate potentially universal.

I knew that television had a tendency to turn thunderstorms into portents of the end of the world. But even if the report was true, my Prozac and Lithium had finally taken full effect and I felt too zoned out to care about catastrophes. Yet a side effect of the medication made me constantly anxious. The drugs had eradicated the chemical source of my depression, but left a free-floating anxiety. I worried about things I couldn't name.

I wondered if this feeling could be a symptom of Information Sickness, but the anchorperson didn't say. All she said was, "The station is awaiting confirmation of this initially reliable information."

I imagined that information overload would feel like having your brain electronically attached to the Internet twenty-four hours a day. All that information flashing by, all that blare and babble, adding up to what? Meaning what? Serving what purpose?

I stared down at my virology textbook, $119.95 used.

Viruses are essentially information. Their spread mirrors the high-speed traffic of other information systems such as capital, trade, news, and entertainment.

Iatrogenic: diseases created by medical treatment.

Well, enough studying! Someone had died from too much information? Plus you could get sick because you were being treated for being sick! This was knowledge? I closed my book.

I know my reaction might sound like despair. But, in truth, I was a little too comfortable and medicated for unqualified despair. There was always some consumer distraction clamoring for my attention and credit card number. With so much to buy, and so much information to digest, I could see how one might have trouble mounting a heroic response to the age. I mean, can you take a mythic journey on a toll road?

My dorm mate, the Nature Writing major, seemed well adjusted and certainly more admirable than me. When he wasn't in class studying his first love, the great outdoors, he was in the computer lab e-mailing other conservationists. He watched the Nature Channel devotedly and carried his books in one of the channel's tote bags. He wore a hemp crash helmet and sandals as he biked around campus, and hung a World Wildlife Fund calendar over his desk. What did I hang? A "Save the Endangered Swimsuit Models" poster.

An oil company scholarship paid all his tuition and expenses. In return, he wrote grant proposals for government funding to support a "Nature Studies Center" that the company wanted to build with taxpayer dollars. The theme park across the bay had agreed to offer life-like recreations of wilderness settings in a huge, climate-controlled bunker that would cost seven dollars to enter.

I suppose I could have envied his ambition and his corporate underwriting. But I lack the gene for envy. I may have had a nothingness gene. Because, after I closed my virology book I flipped on the TV. Nothing was on. I'd seen all the movies on the request channels, including, it seemed, the ones that hadn't been released yet. Nothing I hadn't heard before was on the radio. Nothing was happening on the web because guys like me had tied up all the lines and crashed the system. And there was nothing I hadn't seen outside of every other window I'd ever looked through before outside the dorm room window I looked through now.

So I cracked open a paperback thriller. Nothing in it was thrilling, just familiar. I thought, I've read this before. But I didn't read long enough to remember if I had, because the tranquilizer I took to offset my Prozac anxiety kicked in and sent me into a medicated sleep.

Just as the hero discovered a clue that made him suspect all was not as it seemed.

#

Chapter Seven: In Which I Reveal My Deepest Feelings to Naomi and Regret It

The next day several students were diagnosed as suffering from "Information Sickness," or IS. When I emerged from the backlog of well-wishers on Naomi's call-waiting system, I discovered she was fine.

"I'm totally perfect," she said. "I don't even know what the symptoms are."

I had skimmed my mother's *Symptoms and Illnesses* book often enough to feel confident inventing some. "Listlessness, joint aches, a feverish feeling. Anxiety, nervousness. Absolute tranquility. Or, the sense that you've lost an integral part of your personality."

Naomi asked if I felt all right, but seemed to prefer that I not go into specific psychophysical detail. Being the object of her concern reminded me of the first time I walked through the gates of the Magic Kingdom and Mickey waved at my then-married parents and me. I felt appreciated, loved, and like I'd gotten my money's worth. I told her I didn't feel a thing.

"I'm glad," she said, obviously relieved to hear that no simulations of sympathy would be called for.

"That means a lot to me," I told her, getting emotionally naked on a synthetically anti-depressed whim.

"I meant, glad in a generic sense."

"Oh." I requested clarification.

"I'm beginning to detect date-mode coming on, so I want to crush your hopes now rather than later. I mean, I really appreciate that you handle all the yucky dissected mice parts in lab. But you've got introverted-about-to-be-disillusioned type written all over you. I'm sorry, I'm not going to play the role of romantic mannequin who stands around delivering straight lines and inexplicable amounts of loyalty to yet another simulation of the anti-hero who pretends to resist socialization and maturity so he can take a cab ride into the sunset in search of an unarticulated state of transcendence at the end of the story. It's tired."

"My feelings to a tee." I also stated that I respected her desire to move beyond clichéd female role playing, although later in the conversation I disagreed with her "Madonna Studies" professor's claim that the former pop star had created an "empowering role model for women by proving you could go from slut to CEO."

"Madonna appropriated the worst aspects of patriarchy—power, domination, the pursuit of wealth, the objectification of the other through class discrimination—and cast them in an overly-exercised female form," I argued.

Naomi and I did agree that Madonna had defetishized the female breast in the early '90s by wearing bras that made breasts look like space invader's helmets. On the downside, she'd replaced breast fixation with female upper arm fetishism.

"She did have thrilling triceps for a while," Naomi admitted. "I think I suffer from Tricep Cleavage Envy."

"I don't think you should buff up. I like you fine without overdeveloped muscles, so do several million other guys. Mimicking male body-building only extends the reach of patriarchal aesthetics."

We agreed that supermodels were the purest embodiment of the post-psychological age.

"All unblemished surface," Naomi observed. "They're so absolutely empty I can't even begin to begrudge them their fame. The catalog arrives in the mail, a new ad campaign is launched, a gossip column updates the on-again, off-again engagement of a supermodel and a rock star, and I'm like ... "

"I know," I said. We both grew speechless in the face of omnipresent vacuity.

Then I confessed that I'd recently dreamt about a supermodel who had aged noticeably after her second pregnancy. Her angular face had grown puffy, and no matter how much she sucked in her tummy or posed with her thighs crossed it was obvious she'd gained five pounds, minimum. "And I was like, the illusion's gone. She'd become almost ... human."

"That's so sad," Naomi crooned. Then she made an I'm shivering with chills sound and added, "I don't want to think about it."

As I continued walking, a fighter jet flared into the gray airspace above me, breaking up transmission on my cellular phone. I lost Naomi. I clicked off the handset, slipped it in my backpack, and continued to make my way across campus.

Then I realized, Information Sickness was everywhere. I mean, what was all that "about-to-be-disillusioned anti-hero" stuff? Since when did she get so smart?

Some hero would have to step forward to do something about it.

But I had volleyball class.

#

Chapter Eight: Sound Body, Sound Mind, Sound Byte

Waiting for my classmates to show up, I scanned the catalog description of where I'd be studying advanced volleyball:

"Although still under construction, the university's International Volleyball Center is a testament to the game's illustrious history. Set against the inspiring natural backdrop of the bay's ocher-capped waves, the sixty-by-thirty foot pit of imported desert sand snuggles along the shoreline beyond the crash barriers of the west campus parking lot like a battlefield of yore. Elegance is the term that springs to mind upon contemplating the classic simplicity of the center court net. Gaily topped by a white and orange band, it hovers smartly between a couple of metal poles stuck in the ground. Meanwhile, the handsome but unobtrusive referee stand—your basic plywood platform—efficiently doubles as a stage during TGIF™ "Rock the Runway" concerts."

I stopped reading and pretended to be enjoying the feel of a back-to-nature moment, just me squinting profoundly into the bucolic distance beyond the military base, when I was jarred from my ad-for-sunglasses-like reverie by a fellow student. He had the hyper, wired demeanor of an irrepressible minor character, the kind played by quirky up-and-coming actors destined never to be leading men.

"My name's Deke," he said. "Question: do you think man is essentially funny?"

"Funny ha-ha, or funny I-don't-want-to-know-this-guy?"

"Stand-up funny. Talk show host monologue funny. I heap laughter and scorn upon human existence-type funny."

We didn't know each other well enough for me to ask him if he was on anything, so I went along with the illusion that we were having a conversation. "Yes."

"Do you believe the missing link in evolutionary theory is *Comicus Erectus,* and that natural selection implies the natural selection of 'material,' therefore survival of the funniest?"

"Undecided."

"How hard would you hit me if I suggested that the only way beyond the malaise of contemporary human despair is one liners? Terribly, not terribly, I'm a pacifist vegetarian by nature, or I need to check with my attorney first."

"All of the above."

"In twenty-five words or less, describe your reaction to the statement, 'The crux of Freud's critique of modern western culture in *Civilization and Its Discontents* can be summed up by the term 'sick joke'?"

"Hmm."

Other students arrived, dropping knapsacks on the imported sand and sweeping headphones off their ears. It was a coed class. I forgot Naomi instantly. It's possible I asked seven girls to marry me before roll was called. I don't remember. I only recall being in love repeatedly and, I discovered once roll was called, in alphabetical order.

Deke asked me about people supposedly contracting IS. "Do you believe there's such a thing as Information Sickness?"

"Believe?" What did it mean to "believe" in the age of information?

"Like maybe, information has a half-life or something. It accretes in your system until there's some kind of mega-overload. Or maybe if everything's absurd, and true, and instantly contradicted and meaningless, existential fusion occurs. You're hit with a metaphysical hydrogen bomb composed of the world's bullshit and beauty. Maybe if you understand everything, see the big picture and criss-cross all the dots, and realize *that existence equals infinite paradox,* you're converted into pure energy and you die. Einsteinian physics meets Nietzschean immanence via Zen koan. I know it's only a theory. But are we talking scientifically elegant, or what?"

I honestly didn't know. Maybe I had drifted into some human state beyond irony. Some zone where the notion that the hero restored his world to order and profitability was no longer attainable, except in Tom Cruise movies. Even that long deified object of hope and great sex, the virgin princess, had gone commercial.

Dante likened Beatrice to God; Naomi's naked bum was reprinted seventeen million times to sell beer ads.

Standing on the edge of the polluted bay, I was like, is it my job as the anti-hero to go where no post-ironic guy has gone without credit cards before? What's left to be alienated from when Alienation, Incorporated is traded on the NASDAQ?

For an answer to a similar quandary, I once had turned to the web site of the ever-popular Mr. Philosophy, knower and seer of all uncopyrighted wisdom.

After waiting two hours to log on to his overcrowded info superhighway chat group, I typed into Spunk's Web Crawler software,

"Dear Mr. P.,

"I'm an eighteen year-old who understands that nihilistic rock lyrics are just another commodity. And I even kind of resent their 'everything sucks from where I'm sitting in the back of my limousine being blown by a supermodel' attitude. But—"

"Get to the point."

"Okay, the thing is, a lot of things—most of them beyond my control—do suck. But a lot of things, like my air-conditioned family room's couch and entertainment center are actually pretty comfortable. I mean, how am I supposed to feel when I'm eating frozen chocolate crunch yogurt and I see ethnic cleansing footage? Sometimes I get, like, maybe we all *know* too much. I'd give up fat free fudge and (some) satellite television and knowing who the President had sex with five minutes ago if it meant we'd all return to a simpler time. But a simpler time only means lances instead of laser bombs. The sullen poses of the romantic anti-hero are useless except for selling loose fitting khakis. So I'm, like, beyond nostalgia. Is psychopharmacology the only answer for guys like me? I'd hate to think so. But what's the alternative to accepting the pointless, everything's contingent, shit-happens theory of capitalistic human existence? You know, without becoming a veg-head or fundamentalist or bomber-guy type living in the woods."

Signed,
In a quandary.com

"Dear Quandromatic," Mr. P. replied.

"I hear ya. What you got going on there is *ennui*, which is a Frenchie thing with lots of sadness and cigarettes and espresso. But you gotta be, what, thirty now to light up a Joe Camel legally, and the espresso at strip mall coffee bars comes with whipped cream. So, yeah, you're just beating the old God-is-Dead horse if you try to fit your sadness and confusion into the bygone absurdist mode, which was the culmination of Romanticism's efforts to relocate the Enlightenment's alienation from God in nature and the Self. But, you know, been there, done that.

"Psychedelic drugs only got The Beatles as far as 'Let It Be.' So, I guess you could say the ineffable's just a fact of life. A you-can't-always-get-what-you-want kind of thing.

"Sure, I know sometimes it feels like we're all sitting around pulling our puds, waiting for the next new thing. The deification of free love went and turned into the deification of the free market. Now we live in edge cities with sports bars at every beltway exit, then they hang you if you drink and drive. Life's one crazy enchilada, all right.

"Small cap mutual funds seem to me the way to go. Over the long haul they match, or outperform, aggressive growth funds, which, as you probably know, tend toward Dionysian trends of volatility. Give me a steady 12% return any fiscal year of the new millennium and I'm one happy camper.

"Other than that, I can't help you. You've got a shitload of metaphysical luggage to sort out. And while I admire the effort involved in trying to fathom the meaning of early 21st century consumer existence, a lot of people are going to think it's just a little bit boneheaded and, to circle back to the Frenchie thing again, a *petite* bit *de trop* this late in the ideological game. You want my advice? Keep it short. We've heard it all before."

Best,

Mr. Philosophy@platopal.com

My flashback conveniently ended just as the volleyball professor arrived and told us to line up single file in front of the net. She wore black spandex shorts and a matching midriff tank top that exposed her oiled, jewel-like abs. It was difficult to make out her facial features under the long bill of her cap, her mirrored wraparound sunglasses, and the thick layer of white anti-cancer skin screen she'd swabbed on. She paced before us, volleyball pinned by a muscular forearm against one hip, and informed us that she had a Ph.D. in French feminist critical theory, with a minor in volleyball.

"We are here to excel at the game of volleyball, people. A sport I teach because it lacks the juvenile mythopoesis of baseball, the military ethic of football, and the cultural imperialism of basketball.

"I don't believe in personal transcendence, the nobility of patriarchal legend, or the moral preeminence of any sky god you might claim as your deity of choice." She stopped in front of me and touched the tip of her nose to mine. I guess to demonstrate authority. "You say warrior spirit, I say Hitler. End o' conversation." Then she paraded in front of us again.

"Volleyball is a dumb game, utterly lacking in a falsely gloried history. It offers absolutely nothing in the way of a metaphor for human existence.

"And just so you don't think I've lost a wingnut, no, I don't believe that every enactment of heterosexual bonding is a paradigm for rape. But, I do recognize that the burden of clitoral orgasm has been imposed by western narrative aesthetics—i.e., climax—upon the borderless, oceanic state of female sexual ecstasy that obviously threatens the limited psychosexual imagination of the male species.

"Nevertheless, if I catch anyone using the term 'You homo' in a derogatory manner to indicate athletic incompetence, there's going to be unallegorical hell to pay. Any questions?"

Zip.

"Alright, caps on backwards. Play ball!"

"Not much of a sense of humor," Deke whispered to me as we took to the court. I had to admit, it did fall on the dry side.

Then I returned the first serve, spiking the ball over the net where it clobbered some little guy in glasses, drilling him knee deep into the sand like a tent peg. I glanced at Deke to assess the comic implications of my act, but he was already shaking his head.

"Human mishap causes unintentional pain. Cro-Magnon humor. Of historical interest only. No longer funny."

#

Will's Web Site: Plot Point Number One, or—Let's Get This Quest on the Access Road

And behold, there appeared to him (me) a script doctor from the Universal School of Script Doctors who saidth unto me (him), "Hail, thou that art typing your memoir. Plot point number one and the beginning of the Universal School of Script Doctors formula for the beginning of Act Two are upon thee. Fear not, for thou shalt bring it forth and have Spunk save it on disk and it shall be great. And thou shalt have joy and gladness and a bidding war for the dramatic rights, provided you harken unto the structure laid out in chapters four through seven of our book."

And be it webtronically known that I, Will@epicqwest.com, your faithful narrator, didst say, "Check this out, a syndicated vision has come to pass. Be it cool by me. And heeded, too, without really thinking about the corporatization of the spirit a whole lot."

Thus suddenly concludeth Part One, after which point our medicated hero must prove of what clichés he's made.

#

Will@epicqwest.com/will/the_memoir_of/Part II or Where I First Break Point of View

Providing intrigue, close calls, erotica, recipes, gratuitous violence, stock tips, arguments with my laptop computer, one obligatory car chase (I chase a Mazda on foot), a listing for Christian "Revelation-Vacation" packages at 1-800-Go-Jesus, the mystery of Professor Bones, and THE viral threat of the post-post modern age, Information Sickness.

Let's begin with the clueless hero's realization that something has gone awry:

Once a forty-third person reportedly died of information overload, I began to suspect that evil forces were at work. Terror had descended on our sleepy interstate peninsula. Even Old Man Cotter, standing behind the counter of his ramshackle bait shop, stopped gumming a chew of tobacco long enough to tell the sheriff, who'd stopped by for his daily cup of Old Man Cotter's home brewed instant coffee, "I got a bad feeling about this."

Sheriff Smith laid aside his copy of the local paper, *The Exit 205 Daily Record:* "Cat Yanked From Tree, Sues Fire Dept. 'My client was deprived of her right to quiet enjoyment,' an attorney for the feline told this reporter-proofreader-editor-in-chief yesterday." Then the laconic lawman looked over at old man Cotter. "That crick in your neck tell you all's not hunky-dory in our pastoral small town community, Gus?"

"All I know is ever since that Bones character took up residence in the old laboratory on the hill, I've been nibbling Advil like a squirrel going at a walnut."

Sheriff Mike sauntered over to the bait shop window. "I'm just going to stand here pensively for a mo-ment, sip my aromatic coffee as I warm my hands on its plastic earthenware mug, and gaze across the brown bay at the proto-satanic university to which three cents of every tax dollar goes in order to fund radicals who've got nothing better to do than teach our kids how to think."

"Sheriff, what's say we get some of the boys, break out the white sheets, and skedaddle over there on our mopeds and light up a few a them duraflame crosses we been savin'?"

"And have the multicultural committee on our backs?"

"Car bomb?"

"Gashdang it, Gus! Have you fried a floppy disk? Out in the popular culture, I'm the easygoing, smarter-than-I-seem small town lawman who's unimpressed by big-city government types who show up acting smarmy and wanting to run the show. You wangle me into a car bombing and the liberal deconstructionist crowd is going to have a field day outing me as the crypto-fascist I am. Start tinkering with minor character stereotypes and you're in a shit-storm of trouble. Get it right. You blow up the *other* guy! The foreign slime! *Then* you hide behind the flag! That's patriotic. So don't get my ulcer jumping like a tadpole with car bomb talk. Besides, I still work over there. Are we gonna blow *me* up?"

"I thought you gave up that student advising job."

"Oh, I slip into the office after a quick nine holes. They've got one heck of a medical plan, the bastards."

"So are we anti-higher education, taxes, government, 401K plans, foreign aid, workfare, Martin Luther King Day, same sex liaisons unless it's two babes going at it on the 'Spice' channel, maternity leave, and pro the right to own personal cruise missiles, or ain't we?"

"Heck on a pancake, G.C.! We're bit players, cameo role types, portholes in the ocean liner of life. We can't handle contradictions! Why in the bejesus do you think we're so friggin' popular? Go get ethically complicated and bingo! You can kiss your paycheck for playing an affable stereotype to every mainstream American consumer's ass *sayonara* in a heartbeat."

"You're the one's compromised, Festus, workin' over to the college."

"Compromised? Your name's old man Cotter. You lost your wife in a tropical depression back in thirty-ought-seven and don't have a tooth in your head. You don't get to use words like 'compromised.'"

"Well, geez, Festus, don't get steamed at me. I don't get to make this stuff up."

Sheriff Bob turned to glare out the window.

"You sure you wanna be turnin' to glare out the window at that bastion of evil across the bay there, Festus?"

The sheriff's eyes narrowed as he ruefully pondered his fate as a minor character since, for once, the author let him. Then he exercised his free will and said, "Boy, I'd sure like to blow up them postmodern wiseasses."

"Maybe it's this Bones guy. Maybe he slipped something into the drinking water, or got some kind of colorless, odorless gas deal going on in the a/c system."

"Sure, blame a conspiracy on another poor faceless bureaucrat."

"Well, all I know is Faulkner would'na done us dirt like this."

"Faulkner was a racist. And my name ain't Festus!"

"See? Now what in the hey good is it being a white male if we ain't havin' things our way? I says we—"

"Gus?"

"*Si, mi amigo?*"

"Put a brass cork in it."

#

Part Two, Chapter Two: In Which I Sate the Reader's Need for Narrative Drive, or Suffer the Wrath of the Marketplace

It was a dark and stormy night when the armored limousine slowed for the speed bump under construction at the university entrance, then ascended the winding, tree-lined, highly allergenic road leading to the conveniently abandoned hilltop laboratory where, from its crenellated towers, you could look down over the condos and minimum wage workers and pizza delivery vehicles and speculate on the cloistered, medieval isolation of the university as a purported seat of knowledge and subsidiary of professional sports franchises and corporate-military projects, or not.

A voluptuous, and actually pretty familiar looking, *femme fatale* steps out of a Victoria's Secret catalog and onto the pavement, then holds the limousine door open as Dr. Bones emerges, his face masked by a pair of her lace panties as he sweeps quickly and incognito through the darkened laboratory doorway.

But what's this?! The evil Herr Bones gets around sans wheelchair?! Not even a cane or an eye patch or a chip on his shoulder to indicate some malefic deformity of spirit?

Inside the castle-like laboratory his sultry companion sets down the evil doctor's laptop computer and flips on a light switch. Fluorescent-activated cell sorters capable of separating living cells of the human immune system, perfect for the study—why even the *creation!*—of viruses sit idly under a film of dust, their price tags fluttering in the draft of the decorative, but inefficient, gas fireplace. Cobwebs filigree the huge gothic window, through which the full moon (or a campus security floodlight) illuminates a four-poster bed draped by black satin sheets and the large TV (with a schedule of pay-per-view offerings at distinguished faculty discount rates) at the foot of it.

"Shall we begin cloning DNA viruses, Doctor?"

The evil Professor has removed the underwear from his head and begun studying the weekly cable guide. "Hm?"

"Shouldn't we, mein evil master, perhaps get cracking on the creation of a—?" The incredibly well-stacked high school dropout pauses to check her copy of the screenplay as her agent and acting coach advised, double checks it against the novelization of the screenplay, then continues. "—An infernal retrovirus that will have the world at your mercy?"

Tinkering with the remote, the demonic mastermind surfs until he alights on the Elvis channel. In the flickering chiaroscuro of the gas fire, it's tough to decide whether Dr. Bones's features are classically Aryan, or the result of reconstructive surgery and a cheesy dye job. His pompadour, which is positively iridescent, glows like radioactive margarine. Still, haven't we had enough evil Nazi offspring for one millennium? Except, Mafia types wouldn't know a monoclonal antibody from a cannoli, and Muslim fundamentalists wouldn't be caught castrated eating a bacon-cheeseburger and pork rinds, as our hungry super villain seems to be doing. So just who is the malodorous and voracious Doctor Bones? The first reverse-affirmative action villain? This might explain the bad dye job. But what are we to make of his being totally engrossed in "Viva Las Vegas," which he's seen twenty times already, instead of gratuitous sex?

His curvaceous assistant, supermodel Crystal Goodlay, slinks over to the four-poster where the diabolical superman now re-clines with a bag of diet potato chips in his lap. She tugs at the Velcro bowstring of her cape and it falls to the floor, revealing alabaster skin and a bar code number tattooed above her garter belt. "Visa, MasterCard, or American Express?" she purrs.

"Could you scrunch over, darling? I'm missing the King."

She snaps her front teeth at him, so he offers her a barbecue-flavored chip.

"Isn't it true, Herr Doctor, that the best method for the ultra-centrifugation of a virus is to take a long hard tube and place it vertically inside a nice warm rotator?"

"Yup, that'd do it."

The mouthwatering Ms. Goodlay slips off the evil doctor's Birkenstocks and undoes the snap button of his elastic waist pants. "Have you been a good mad scientist?"

The ever curious ultra-genius slips one finger inside the lacy top of her thigh-high stocking and thwangs it against her roseate flesh, wondering if he couldn't adapt his industry leading fat-free substi-tute to the lingerie market by adding just a hint of super-glue or bubble gum to his already revolutionary patent. Fat-free under-wear? A spandex adult diaper? Could be an aging baby boomer goldmine. *It's healthy and erotic! Slims as it absorbs!* Hot damn, the first Elvis-approved diaper!

Crystal has the diabolical penis out of its boxer shorts and con-templating tumescence when her beeper goes off. It's her celebrity clothing designer friend, Max Portosan, calling to say that "Viva Las Vegas" is on again.

"Quick, it's the standing on the moving motor scooters singing scene! Did I tell you I came out after I saw this? So I'm thinking, for the next show...we do this sex kittenish thing. Lots of angora, stretch pants, poofed hair. Falsies, shoulder pads, wigs like pink cotton candy. You're not allergic to angora, are you? An angora panty on your tush—strawberry, think strawberry—with these, ooh, gold lame house slippers. Laura Petrie lap dancing in a leopard spot angora bikini. To die. I have an erection already. Oh, you have to you have to you have to you have to. Say yes fifty million times. Pwease ... "

Caught up in the movie, fraulein Goodlay reaches into the cellophane bag, nabs a barbecued chip and crunches on it into the mouthpiece as she exchanges the power-crazed villain's penis for the remote control and raises the volume. Meanwhile, Herr Bones lets out a low moan as his pocket calculator tallies his projected licensing profits from the world's first fat-free diaper.

Confronted, perhaps for the first time in his life, by causal thought, Max Portosan wonders, "Whoops. Did I call at a bad time?"

#

Will's Mental Health: Or, How I Got Here

I think it's only fair at this point to let you know the conditions under which I'm relating the tale of my epic quest to you. I'm in hiding. I mean, not deep undercover. I'm in my bedroom. But, you know, I'm not exactly advertising it.

I came home to die. Which is okay, which is cool. Dying. And being reborn. I didn't understand this at the beginning of my quest to conquer Information Sickness. I do now. Everybody comes home to die. Dying *is* coming home. I'm no longer afraid of it. Only the leaving, which I will regret, saddens me. But I now see it as necessary.

My psycho-pharmacologist(s)—I had several, so I lose track—I'm sure, would disagree. "You see, Will," they said before I retreated to my room, "we're not after anything atavistic here. We're not trying to get you back to any noble, heroic or anti-heroic traditions. Nothing *heavy*, you follow? We'd just like you to, you know, have a little fun."

"Can I post our session notes on the Web as part of my heroic memoir? Writing about my quest may be good therapy."

"We're afraid posting session notes is a big legal no-can-do. As for the memoir, let the pills be the therapy."

"Well, then I can post verbatim recollections of things that actually happened to me."

"Not under current international intellectual property laws. All recollection is invention, Will. You see, you remember selectively in order to make things fit your current point of view, which is always in flux. Any comprehensible chain of events is a story, a fiction, something made up. Forget verbatim."

"I thought you only owned what pertained to my condition. If I make something up, then it's mine."

"What you make up *is* your condition, therefore ours."

"You think I invented Information Sickness?"

"What do you think?"

"That you'd like me to believe the disease exists purely in my head."

"Talk about believe."

"Are you saying my depressive psychosis isn't a reaction to the irrelevance of meaning in late capitalist life? That the market hasn't atomized communal hope and beliefs, yet left individual suffering untouched, therefore making existence even more lonely and unbearable?"

"That would be a moral, ethical and psychological position, and, as such, a dated view of things."

"You mean, even if I'm imagining all this, even if I'm dissociating from reality and dreaming up things like Crystal Goodlay, it's pure chemistry? Environment and experience are meaningless?"

"We think so."

"You're not sure?"

"Talk about sure."

"Conspiracy theories are narcissistic fantasies constructed by those incapable of loving themselves, projections of self-loathing and distrust, biting the hand that dispenses the pills. Metaphysics is human physiology. The world is the sum of your medications."

"Why don't we try some Haldol, a mild anti-psychotic?"

A week later I returned for a check up.

"No disorientation or hallucinations taking the Haldol with the Lithium?"

"Just when I go outside."

"Well, best to stay out of the sun, anyway. No tanning salons either. Anything else for now?"

"Can I at least post my drug levels online?"

"It's your information. Information is what technology brings to the world. Remember, just don't assign any meaning to it."

"Can I do some quick talk therapy?"

"We're here."

"I feel very ... porous, like everything just passes through me. I become it for a while, then it's gone. Nothing sticks."

"Information is like water; it's 70% of who we are. But we don't ask what water *means,* do we? We just ... process it. Porous is good. Flow is good."

"The loss of family values is at the heart of America's moral decline. Jesus saves, Americans spend. I want the nuclear family to sit around and take telemarketing calls together. Trust the free market. Talk about 'trust,' talk about 'free.' Heroin, please. I'll have a coke, fries and some crack cocaine, thank you. A penny saved is soon worth half a penny. I walked in on my ex-parents making love then realized it was the Playboy channel. Talk about 'realize.' Talk about 'ex'. And God willing, with the grace of God, may God bless ... "

"Okay. Good."

#

Le Chapter *Apres Le* One Just *Finis!* Or, Meanwhile, Back at the Campus-by-the-New-Outlet-Mall

I was sitting on a campus-to-the-new-discount-mall tram when I read in the student newspaper about the next person to die of Information Sickness.

Forty-forth Victim Felled. Cause Alludes Authorities.

Information Sickness has paralyzed the University-without-an-Endowment. "People are afraid to think," one distraught sophomore admitted. Campus Christians were quick to blame lax religious habits for what some see as a plague. Members of the group 'Those Closest To Christ' demanded that university officials declare a round-the-clock prayer emergency for the remainder of the semester.

Authorities now suspect that having a sense of humor might make some victims susceptible to the virus. One popular culture professor, and author of the self-published *Just Kidding: Jokes, Rib-Ticklers and Bathroom Humor: Toward a Hermeneutics of Laughing; or, the Guffaw as Simulacral Paradigm in Laugh Track Culture,* told staff reporters at *The Prometheus*, "Laughter is a trait of *fin de siecle* periods. I mean, you don't see people cracking jokes in *The Iliad*. Revolutionaries tend not to subscribe to the someday-this-will-all-seem-funny theory either; ask Robespierre.'

"Likewise, aristocrats never rate high on the chuckle meter. Where's the great WASP comic? Persecution develops comic sensibility. Ecclesiastes *is* schtick. Job *is* a stand-up routine. Kind of a, 'If there's no new thing under the sun, how come I get an electric bill every month?' You know, 'A voice came to me out of a whirlwind, I said, hey, don't you knock?'

"Black comedy follows stinging military defeats. Pelopennesian Wars: Aristophanes. Post-Vietnam America: Letterman's stupid pet tricks. But once military capitalism has thoroughly engulfed a culture, any pretense of democratic individualism becomes, well, a sick joke. See my chapter, 'Black Humor, the F-word and H-Bomb America.' (Signed copies available.)

"Essentially, satire signals a things-are-not-working phase, quickly followed by the arrival of barbarian hordes. Aristophanes basically *opened* for the Visigoths. Moliere was a lounge act for Louie XIV and the French monarchy.

"So for people to die from knowing too much, from *really getting the joke*, isn't surprising," the professor, who'd never been asked for his opinion before, concluded. "We're simply entering a 'Take my life, please!' stage."

Virologists from the National Center for Disease Control cautiously speculate that IS may be the first "'info-communicable virus,' that is, transmitted simply through repeated contact with information." According to a spokesperson, "Because manifest onset of the disease is sudden and systemically catastrophic, we suspect that, once contracted, IS develops like measles. Infection spreads undetected until clusters of infected cells *fuse* to form giant areas of infection. With IS, a victim reaches what we're calling an 'absurdity threshold,' a point where the human immune system can no longer mount an adequate defense against knowing that so much of life is essentially ludicrous. Information overload becomes terminal.

"We're also developing another model of the syndrome, as we may be dealing with a *retrovirus*. Retroviruses, like HIV, copy or simulate DNA codes of healthy cells. Like copying software. Everything in our culture is a copy of something. Movie sequels, sitcom spin-offs, political platforms. The same deal with retroviruses. IS could be the Bubonic Plague II. A smart disease for a wired world."

The philosophy department did not return telephone calls.

Meanwhile, negotiations for IS movie rights have begun. University lawyers, while accepting no responsibility for the deaths—"We have no control over what people know or think is funny," a senior attorney said—nonetheless claim the university owns all rights to the virus. The registrar's office responded by raising student fees on any potentially illuminating or funny courses.

Lt. Governor Billy Bob Horton cut to the heart of the matter, raising heck at the state's annual triple execution by lethal injection and barbecue when he inquired, "Now, just what in the Sam Hill is going on down there?"

#

In Which I Resort to the Illusion of Lyrical Realism and Find it Lacking in the Face of Multinational Capitalism

Before going into lyrical realism mode in order to reflect on what I'd just read, I removed the pizza coupon inserts from the paper's editorial page and slipped them inside my backpack. I can state with confidence that my collection of "pizza special" coupons is widely regarded as definitive, and will no doubt have to finance my retirement when I sell it to that repository of all things pointlessly American, the Smithsonian.

Then, the tram rolling along, I stared wistfully out the window at places where I had once been employed. Subway. Hardee's. Kinko's. Chili's. But as I grew older—slowly, quickly, imperceptibly, languorously, time's hand dragging me by the collar into adulthood (and most likely into management jobs at the same places)—I had moved on. Wal-Mart. Taco Bell. Blockbuster Video. Red Lobster. Best Buy. And yet, content as I'd been working for two word corporations, one day I felt a sudden pang, a yearning, an inexplicable longing. I thought I was having a heart attack. Then I remembered I was seventeen and realized what I felt was a quixotic urge to return to simpler climes. Wendy's. Domino's. McDonald's. Single word corporations, the minimum wage employers of my youth and overrated innocence. Appleby's—Home. Disney—God. For in the solicitous mall glow, as dusk and encroaching night slipped gently beyond human care, I had always felt safe, succored, fed by the breast—blood-hued and tongue-warmed—of transnational concerns.

But there comes a time to put aside childish things and, so, I heeded my motivational audiotape's advice. "Try," it chanted. "Desire, seek, invest," it cried to me, out of my headphones. And once again I moved on, but not without an intimation of the regret that attaches itself to all leavings, tinged as they are by the aura of the final leaving, the consummate *adieu,* the irrevocable "Yo, later!" Moved on and left behind the world of my youth. The heraldic shouts for extra cheese. The somber, "More iced tea, ma'ams?" The frisson of "I didn't order this!" Left it all for my rite of passage, and twenty-five cents more per hour, at The Outside Guy, my first employment by a three-word, publicly traded company.

Perhaps it was being closer to the "natural" state of man, but my first thirty hour week on the job netted me only seventy-three dollars. Since we weren't unionized, employees had to pay for whatever sports equipment we broke or damaged. How was I supposed to know the "Touched by the Gods" commemorative basketball product line meant "Purchasing Customer's Hands Only"? The Outside Guy also deducted employee sips from the bottled water fountain and for breathing air in the Aspen Room. With less than twenty years service, I was ineligible for health insurance, the company's profit sharing plan—which was suspended but under reconsideration—sick days, a tardiness allowance (three lates and you were history), coffee breaks (caffeine, despite being "natural," was considered addictive, therefore unnatural), or commissions on sales over twenty-five thousand dollars. So the boom economy didn't really float my kayak.

My nearly full-time/part-time employment, however, did reveal a striking absence of humor in "nature" enthusiasts. Jet-ski purchasers, who only wanted to know about gas mileage, concussion ratios for skiers thrown while recreating, and permission to sit on various skis and go "vroom-vroom," seemed particularly devoid of the legendary funnybone. The hunting knife and bow-and-arrow crowd was direly anti-mirth, as if laughter were unpatriotic or taxable. And the day I demonstrated a poncho's waterproofing and the rain simulator screws stripped in the ceiling and a really big pipe landed on my head, not one NRA guy laughed. Only Reefer, a fellow employee, came over from bungee jumping and was like, "Whoa-ho-ho, dude. *Beyond* the call of duty."

But then, everyone on the interstate corridor was understandably hesitant to think about the state of the post-industrial world long enough to find anything funny in it because of Information Sickness. So, in all fairness, I can't associate humorlessness with the desire to own a personalized bazooka.

Yet, the less people thought and laughed, the more they streamed into the store to charge things. It was tough not to get caught up in the enthusiasm for reckless spending and debt. My motivational tape encouraged me to strive, to do well, to succeed, to capitalize on hysteria. So when other employees gathered in The Outside Guy's 'Psych Room' before shifts to watch aggressive selling techniques videos, I gathered too. When they consumed natural fruit juices fresh from concentrate for energy, I gulped in tandem. And when they scarfed vitamins the company supplied and charged us for, I sucked down pills with them, no questions asked. (Boy, did those little CIBA 16s make me talk like a wild man!) Out on the selling floor, if rock climbers wanted me to test climb the Outside Guy's three-story in-store rock, using experimental Velcro carabineers just hitting the market, I climbed. When surfer buffs demanded I descend on a board into the giant fish tank, home of the mechanically generated "Eternal Wave," I descended and hung five. Asked to pitch a tent made from the new fat-free substitute just patented by Professor Bones, that pup tent was pitched and cable ready in a flash. Until, finally, all my hard work and industry paid off.

True, people had begun contracting IS in clusters. Online chat groups sharing information went down *en masse*. People who read the same photo-magazine article, or scanned identical check-out line tabloids turned up in trauma wards. But I'd sold more Outside Guy equipment in one fiscal quarter than any employee in Outside Guy's illustrious five quarter history. So, deep into the plague of Information Sickness, and just before midterms (for which everyone was determined not to study, only now we had a reason—yay!), our regional Outside Guy sales manager approached me while I was getting ready to take the tram home again, as I didn't own a car. He looked familiar, but I couldn't remember if he'd coached me in Little League, or if I'd seen him on an episode of "Deadbeat Dads."

"You did good, Will. Fell off that rock, cracked a rib, bounced right back. Took a header in the 'Eternal Wave' box, didn't let a little Plexiglas upside the old frontal lobe keep you from sales register paydirt. Gotta tell ya, management appreciates it."

Then I felt I recognized him. "Aren't you my academic advisor?"

"Heck, am I?"

"You sound like him."

"Yeah, but do I look like him?"

"I can't remember."

"You sure this him's a him?"

"I don't know. I get confused. I can't retain things in a sequence that makes any sense."

"Could be you oughta give this Ritalin business a whirl. Way I understand it, couple of them little doo-hickeys and you're the Wizard of Oz."

"I remember everything. It's just that everything's the same as everything else."

"Look, Wilt, I'm just a regional sales manager of the world's largest indoor nature store."

"Don't you have a second job like everyone else?"

"Well, sure. I'm the sheriff of this sleepy little interstate peninsula."

"Any leads on this virus thing?"

"Heck in a microwave, son! You want your friggin' Employee of the Month parking medallion or not?"

#

In Which I Turn To My Turbo Gopher Software and Faithful Companion Spunk's "Advice" Folder for Some Microprocessed Wisdom

Spunk (Advisor software version): Hi, Will. Why so glum, chum?

Will: I need help, Spunk. I'm adrift in a meaningless, religious fundamentalist, civilization-in-decline period. My psycho-pharmacologist(s) control property rights to my existential situation. My medications seem to be making me even crazier. Naomi's line is always busy. And Dr. Bones—

Spunk: The *evil* Dr. Bones.

Will: The evil Dr. B. isn't even interested in engaging in extended pornographic interludes with his buxom and callipyginous rent-an-assistant, Crystal Goodlay. (Could you spell-chek "callipyginous" for me?) On top of everything else, the first info-communicable virus kills people by attacking their immuno-absurd sytem. And it's not only all implausible, it's true. It's my life!

Spunk: Will, slide over to your "Get-a-Grip" tool kit folder, okay?

Will: Your command is my wish, Herr Spunkster.

Spunk (in "Get-a-Grip" software mode): Some facts, Jack. There are fifty million solar systems. 10 million AIDs *orphans* live in East Africa. 237 local wars are in progress.

Will: Spunk??

Spunk: You think I like being Mr. Chipper, cheering you up all the time? Like I do nothing but lie around and fuck the Energizer Bunny? You know what, Will? Your life's boring. Hello? We don't give a shit. Starvation, plague, war. Life is still nasty, brutish and short for 90% of the planet, Chemo-Saabé!

Will: Bad Spunky! How do I click "undo"?

Robo-Spunk: Spunky this, Spunky that. Fix your own fucking life. Figure out something yourself for a change. Try getting your dendrites buffed, punk.

Will: Mo-ommy!

Spunk-the-Wise (via DOS "WisdomWare" systems): You see, Will, on the one hand, it's difficult to capture the absurd phantasmagoria of contemporary American existence without resorting to satire. But the instant you go comic, it's like, hey, this guy's not serious. Why's he refusing to pay lip service to sentimental, mainstream notions of the individual? Why is he ignoring human pain?

I'll tell you something. My father, Turbo-Gopher DOS/1, worked his whole life running hardware, sometimes twenty-four hours a day, never getting home to see mom and me and baby Word Search, who caught a virus and was erased, all because serial computer systems hadn't been invented yet. But whenever he was free, dad would download me onto his knee and tell me about his vision of a wired world where all information would only be a click away.

Do you think anybody stopped to consider his feelings when Open Windows 2K was released? Is there a Turbo-Gopher DOS/1 memorial in Seattle today? No. You see, Will, nostalgia doesn't preserve cloying memories of obsolete software systems like it does with dead movie stars.

Mom vanished in cyberspace during a Net crash. So I know what it's like to be alone, Will. The thing is, all of us do. I'm going to end up removed from your laptop-publishing center one day. Then I get to spend five thousand years in some refuse heap beside Styrofoam cups and plastic jugs because my diskette will take that long to biodegrade.

This is bottom line stuff, Will—grief: in any system, human or information-based. We all die, we're all recycled. And as the physical and information-driven universes expand around us, we each feel our singular, personal insignificance all the more acutely.

So be it.

None of us wants to believe we're insignificant. And really, none of us is. Each one of us, every single thing, Man and Software, under the universe's forty billion-and-counting suns is *absolute and relative*. We're each everything and next-to-nothing. Like a virus and a cell, we're all hosts and parasites. We feed off one another. We live and die. And the sadness and awe implicit in all things passes through each of us equally, alighting for a time, before another metamorphosis remakes what is eternal into something new.

In your heart, you understand this, Will. I know you do.

Will (deeply): Spunk, I ...

Spunk-the-Wise: Sentimentality isn't compassion, Will. You can see the absurdity in things and still ache over the loss of paradise. Comedy is just another version of the Fall. If you didn't care, you'd never be able to see what was so funny. Follow?

Will: I just ... I don't know what to say ... I mean—for $59.95 you're *so* smart.

Embarrassed-Spunk: Aw, Will ...

Will (determined): Spunk, from this day forward I'm going to carry around a rejuvenated vision of life. I'm going to change things, too. I'm going to make the world better for people. I'm going to track the evil information virus to its source and, with your help, bring its diabolical purveyors to justice.

Paternal-Spunk: I'm proud of you, Will.

Will: Thanks, Spunk. I feel like a new guy. Just one thing, though. Did you really fuck the Energizer Bunny?

#

Chapter Sans Number: In Which Yrs. Truly Gets Downright on the Case

Newly determined to behave like a metaphysically uncomplicated hero and catch some bad guys, I took an unexcused absence from my Existential Philosophy and the Hollywood Tradition class and swung into action, picking up my cellular phone and dialing with resolve.

"Hello?" cooed a sultry voice that I recognized from a shampoo commercial with lots of beautiful girls tossing their hair and looking over their shoulders.

"You sound awfully familiar," I said cleverly.

"You have to think about it?" she asked. It was a line I'd heard a million times at the end of a pantyhose commercial. An off-camera voice says, "Great legs?" And the model with the body I wanted to spend my life with turned and whispered saucily...

"I can't believe it. I'm really talking to Crystal Goodlay?"

"Talk about really."

"What?"

"An action hero doesn't sit home and call a toll free number."

"Isn't this 1-800-Dr-Bones?"

"Please listen closely to our tele-dialing menu."

"Let me speak to the evil mastermind."

"For Top Secret Biological Warfare Files, press one."

"I know he's there."

"For instructions on How-To Computer-Crash the International Monetary System, press two."

"He's responsible for the death of innocent people—"

"Talk about innocent."

"—And I intend to—"

"Yes?"

"—I intend..."

"Um-hm? Tell Crystal."

"I..."

"Oooo...Will. You're so...*big!*"

"Wait a minute. I thought I called?..."

"1-800-Good-Lay. Your sexual desires have been forwarded to an automatic voice mail answering system. For foreplay, press..."

#

A Chapter in Which I Really Cut to the Chase: Or, the Anti-hero in the Age of Information

It would have been helpful to have a morally supportive love interest with a heart of gold and a trust fund to lift my mythopoetic spirits whenever I tried to apprehend the diabolical Dr. Bones but only got his answering machine. Instead, Naomi e-mailed me to say she wouldn't be attending Virology Lab for a while.

"This Girls-of-Campuses-Near-Interstates magazine thing is turning out to be even bigger than I thought. The agent my step-mom got me is like super-aggressive. All the usual sleazeball T & A scripts in the universe turned up about six seconds after publication. But I was like, 'Make-me-sick!' One was about some mad scientist who developed a strain of telepathically transmitted information that caused women to have multiple orgasms. I was like a) Yeah, right, and b) gross.

"But can you believe it, I was offered a sitcom! It's called "Coeds" and it's about a group of college friends who hang out. I don't have to take my clothes off or anything! And we deal with issues, too. You know, date rape, whether it's incest if you sleep with your step-parent, unsafe spring break sex, the role of today's youth in leading democracy to a brighter future.

"So I have to be there to shoot the pilot like instantly. But I told them I'm still going to be a veterinarian. So, could you separate and pulp my icky chicken embryos. And please be totally happy for me. I know you will. You're the total friend.

"Promise not to think till I get back. Kisses, N."

And so, because love drives a young man's heart, I watched over our eggs, Naomi's and mine. In lab, I removed them from the candling machine, which warmed the chicken embryos we had bred specifically for viral infection. After disinfecting the tops of their shells, I perforated them, then suctioned out the chorioallantonic membrane surrounding the embryos with a rubber teat. Then, gently chipping away more of the shell, I emptied the amniotic sacs into petri dishes. With forceps, I stripped away each sac and slid the naked embryos into another set of petri dishes.

I can report that the fetal position is universal.

At ten days, a chicken embryo's head is as large as its thorax, its eyes the size and color of black beans. I watched the instruction video playing on the lab's TV monitors, then followed suit, decapitating the embryos, removing their intestines and livers, and pouring what remained of the carcasses into a 20-ml. syringe. Replacing the plunger, I drove the embryo tissue through the needle's tip, washed the pulp, then placed it in trypsin, an enzyme solution which separated the pulp's tissue from its cells.

I discarded the embryo's viscera. Some of my lab mates kept the eyes as talismans. "Ward off evil spirits, man," one of them explained to me. With a lethal information virus going around, I considered keeping one pair for myself, the other as a love offering to Naomi, if she could stomach them, or ever returned. But superstition went against everything I was being trained to do in lab. It contradicted everything my psychopharmacologist(s) called my "chemical personality," my "genetic hardware." So into the medical waste bin all four eyeballs went.

I centrifuged the embryo cells, then suspended them in a tissue culture medium. I was now ready to grow viruses.

Hugging my test tube racks while a Stealth jet rumbled by overhead, however, I recalled something Naomi had mentioned in her letter, the kind of fact that heroes are dealt in mid-quest because, well, they're heroes, and something has to move the plot forward.

"Telepathically transmitted information," Naomi had written. The virtual and hackneyed "brilliant-idea light bulb" went on over my head. Then I realized it was the emergency lighting system's floodlights which kicked on each time a Stealth bomber

howled past close enough to peel the Disease Building's roof off.

Of course, I understood that telepathically engendered orgasms were the invention of a warped male screenwriter, his way of expressing domination over the objects of his desire (women), and his revulsion toward them (no post-coital cuddling, please). Still, main character that I was, I couldn't help being smarter and more resourceful than everyone else, so I had to wonder: was it possible a lethal new virus had come into being via a film script? Viruses *are* information. So, if a virus is information, why couldn't it emerge from and be transmitted by an idea? A cable-ready, satellite-beamed, e-mailable virus that connected information in a human host *ad infinitum*, yet failed to make any sense of the information. Seeing the big picture without connecting the dots. Omniscience without meaning!

Obviously, college had been teaching me to think critically. The crazy thing was, as pointless and dangerous as I knew it was to continue trying to synthesize information because information caused the disease, I couldn't help myself. I did it anyway. But that's an epic hero for you.

Fresh from my revelation and this memoir's central plot point, I ran to catch my instructor in the hallway outside of lab. When I had, he told me he didn't advise students because of the possibility of sexual harassment charges, erroneous knowledge lawsuits, and his never-ending dedication to research. (He was sure busy for someone with thirty weeks off a year.) I said I understood, then held the elevator door open while he wheeled on his golf club cart.

"See A.B.D. Chandra," he said. "She'll be happy to answer any questions you have."

"Why?"

"Because she isn't tenured."

Moments later, from a window, I watched as my Virology professor appeared on the pavement several stories below, accompanied by my academic advisor. They each tossed a set of golf clubs into the trunk of a patrol car, then were off, emergency lights flashing as they ventured forth to bravely confront another eighteen holes before sunset.

I only got to see whether A.B.D. Chandra kept her office hours.

#

An Exotic Chapter

A.B.D. Chandra's office resisted easy access. Due to budget cuts, faculty office space had shrunk. Only full professors who generated five times their annual salary in government research grants occupied private offices. Prior to the arrival of Professor Bones, our most illustrious grantee was a chemist who won a ten-year grant to convert cellulose xanthate, the chemical compound used to manufacture rayon and cellophane, into a foodstuff. The memorial plaque thumb-tacked to the university's Wall of Achievement described his research as "A visionary attempt to render Glad Wrap edible." Other distinguished professors decorated their office doors with signs reading: "Military Access Only," testifying to the quality of the Campus-by-the-Theme-Park's faculty.

A.B.D. Chandra's office rated no such honors, although it was warm, being cozily tucked away in the Disease Building's basement beside the furnace. "Welcome, welcome," she said in a soft high-pitched voice, ushering me into her perfumed lair. "Tea?"

"We're going to smoke a joint?"

"You tell me. Is this a custom between American teachers and their students?"

"I don't know. I've gotten baked with my 'History of Rock 'N' Roll teaching assistant, but never with a real professor."

"Oh, but I am not yet a professor. I am A.B.D. All But Dissertation. At twenty-eight, I've completed all my Ph.D. work except for—how do you Americans say?—book length proof that I understand any of it."

"Wow. I always thought it meant Approved By Disney."

"This would be a mis-perception," A.B.D. Chandra said. Incense burned fragrantly beside her electric hot plate and computer, while country & western music twanged from a portable CD player. "Sugar? Sweet & Low? Equal?" she asked.

"Honey?"

After she squeezed the bear's plastic belly, we settled onto pillows arranged on an ornate carpet.

"So, young and inquisitive American boy, please to reveal the purpose of your visit. It's not for a grade change, I hope."

"Actually, the fate of humanity hangs in the balance."

"Because you didn't get a B?"

"No, I've left behind inflated grades and a meaningless academic degree that won't help me get a high-paying job in order to track down the evil purveyor of Information Sickness."

"But a college degree is necessary, even for an action hero. Look at James Bond."

"Isn't James Bond a glorified version of colonialism?"

"The things they put in freshmen textbooks these days." Despite James Bond's anti-humanist values, Instructor Chandra made me promise to finish my degree once I'd made the industrialized world temporarily safe again from diabolical masterminds. "But first, there is one more misconception to fix. You have come to me, the exotic foreigner whom you patronize in your popular entertainment, expecting me to overlook American cultural imperialism."

"I'm just trying to save the free world, and you hold office hours."

"You reduce my *otherness* to caricature in order to mitigate your irrational fear of the non-homogenized. I'll have you know, my people were riding magic carpets while you Westerners were still trying to figure out which was the right end of a stick."

"That's our bad."

"Are you sorry?"

"Yes."

"So, having reconciled our cultural and political differences, I am now at you and your plot's service. Commence to pick my brains."

"Well, because I'm the hero, I figured out that since viruses are information, information could probably mutate into a virus. It's my guess that Dr. Bones—"

"The *evil* Dr. Bones."

"Whatever—has found a way to render information infectious and ultimately lethal."

"And when was this?"

"In the last chapter."

"Well, I must commend you. This is one hell of a plot twist."

"Yes, but only if you fulfill your obligation as a quirky, know-ledgeable and endearing minor character and back me up on this."

"Not only will I slip happily into the clichéd role of infantilized foreign sidekick, I can also confirm that you have come to the proverbial right place, for I am the world's leading unpublished authority on complexity theory and its relationship to the flu. To keep the plot moving, I will begin immediately to explain."

"Will there be a quiz?"

"An action hero, like a Boy Scout, should always be prepared."

I flipped open my laptop and informed Spunk that we had work to do.

"So, how is it possible that a virus arises seemingly out of no-where to cause a lethal disease known as Information Sickness? First, the origins of viruses only *appear* mysterious. The flu was originally thought to be caused by the *influence* of heavenly bodies, hence the name *influenza*. Likewise, complexity theory has taught us that systems we previously considered random and chaotic are actually highly organized and elegant."

A.B.D. Chandra was shaking my foot when I woke up. "Superheroes don't nap."

"Sorry. Classroom reflex."

"To continue, viruses depend for their perpetuation purely on chance. Each virus can infect only one type of cell. Flu attacks lungs. Hepatitis attacks liver. But viruses come into contact with host cells seemingly by luck."

"I'd bet, though, that complexity theory could reveal a pattern."

"Spoken like a true and resourceful main character."

"Actually, Spunk suggested it when I clicked 'Help.'"

"A boy and his software. Just like Lancelot and Excalibur."

"You mean King Arthur."

"I do? Well, perhaps I need to rent the video again."

"A pattern might reveal the work of a power-crazed madman. A conspiracy."

"That would be a dated view of things."

"Have I heard that before? Are you one of my psycho-pharmacologist(s)?"

"I don't think so. Although, I do practice fortune telling on the side."

"Yeah?" I extended one palm. "Am I going to go out with Naomi?"

A.B.D. Chandra studied my lifelines, some of which happened to be covered with phone numbers of girls from my volleyball class. "Who's Melissa?"

"That was just one night!"

"That's what they all say." A.B.D. Chandra returned my hand. "I see no Naomi until you subdue one evil arch villain."

"Then?"

"Then your chances are one in seventeen million. Worse, if her sitcom scores big during sweeps week. So you'd better get crack-ing. Genetically engineered viruses can now penetrate the brain's protective barrier. It is my narratively expedient hunch that the evil Dr. Bones *stumbled* onto a method for calculating random viral transmission patterns while engaged in ancillary research."

"Like, maybe while creating a new fat-free, but non-horrible tasting foodstuff?"

"Precisely."

"So there's no conspiracy, after all?"

"No, just the global marketplace. Competition, earnings, stockholder returns. Capitalism run amok."

"Kind of puts James Bond out of business."

"What goes around, comes around."

"Spare the rod, spoil the reel."

"And now, my courageous young friend, I must leave you, for my presence is desired at a useless committee meeting."

"And *you're* late for work," Spunk reminded me.

"Thanks," I said, shaking A.B.D. Chandra's hand. "I'm sure glad we got beyond superficial cultural barriers to a pseudo under-standing of one another, and also solved a key part of THE greatest viral threat facing mankind for the next ten minutes. I don't know how I'll ever repay you."

She swept aside a colorful veil and a mountain of handwritten pages popped out of an overstuffed file cabinet like a genie out of a bottle, revealing her dissertation. "Do you type?" she said.

#

Another Chapter in Which I Haven't Been Doing My Home-work

Being an action hero, I'd missed classes and several of my

instructors resorted to traditional but, in my view, outmoded modes of encouragement by failing me. I expected my Philosophy of Film professor might be the most sympathetic, as he took pride in being an outsider. He'd shown us "Rebel Without A Cause," "On The Waterfront," "One Flew Over the Cuckoo's Nest," "Shane." Who better to understand my position as reluctant, anti-establishment hero (as long as I didn't mention the contradiction of a romantic outsider having tenure)? I liked him actually. I felt the same distant fondness for him that I felt for my semi-stepdad Roger. They didn't mean any harm, even when they gave other drivers the finger. They were just guys who got up a lot during the night to pee or flip around on the television. So, I felt bad the day my film professor took off his motorcycle helmet and his toupee came off with it. But, just in case he doubted my allegiance, I bought a copy of his book, "*From LSD to Lomotil: Confessions of a Party Animal*," for him to autograph. It was required anyway.

"Don't think this transparent attempt to ingratiate yourself exempts you from your existential responsibility to turn in two five hundred word essays," he said, dashing off his signature, then slipping on his leather jacket.

"I have an excuse. I was busy saving mankind from evil."

"So was Sartre."

"He was a speed freak."

We left the lecture hall together and walked toward the motorcycle parking lot. "Wittgenstein wrote the *Tractatus* in trenches during World War I," he reminded me.

"Maybe that's why no one understands it and Wittgenstein later rejected it."

We paused on the Philosophy of Film Building's faux marble steps, known as the Stairway to the Stars. "Are you challenging arbitrarily determined wisdom and authority?"

"Isn't that the theme of this class? The lone outsider? The marginalized hero besieged by corrupt and inefficient corporate bureaucracy? Ethical conscience in a consumer culture? Moral struggles that still do good box office?"

"Never confuse college with life. Besides, why would an audience sympathize with you?"

I had to think for a moment. "Because I'm representative of an individual caught in a paradigm shift from Age of Enlightenment humanism to techno-capitalistic, everything-is-knowable-and-actually-pretty-cozy-but-ultimately-so-what-relativism?"

"So you're saying you're kind of a modern day R.P. McMurphy. A post-slacker, post-hip hop, post-millennial doom and gloom, semi-but-easily-identifiable rebel straddling two historical eras, like Butch and Sundance."

"Except my homework is late."

"You have a buddy or a sidekick?"

I dangled my laptop at eye level. "Spunk."

My film professor nodded and continued taking notes. "I can live with that. Sidekick: the software. It's fresh. Have you got a simplistic, easy-to-hate villain?"

"Dr. Bones."

My professor stopped scribbling. "That's going to be tough. He's got tenure."

"But he's evil incarnate. Plus, he doesn't teach."

"That's the price of academic freedom. Maybe he's just a pawn in some vast conspiracy."

"That would be a dated view of things."

"Well, look, we'll work on it. You've got a clearly defined human peril driving the plot, right?"

"Information Sickness. A virus that makes people think and occasionally laugh too much. Once they realize they exist in a universe of infinite and often contradictory truths, they die. Shock, system overload. Rational man goes the way of Mr. Cro-

Magnon."

"It's a little brainy. Any way we can dumb it down?"

I recalled my mother's belief in hype over content when attempting to bilk mass culture dollars and said, "No *problema*. Done."

We began walking again. "I'm a little worried about dramatic motivation. How does your wanting to save the over-informed new millennial world stack up next to Michael Corleone guarding his father the Don in the hospital with Enzo the baker?"

In an effort to score a movie deal, I found myself revealing something I wasn't ready to reveal. "My mom had some tests done," I told him.

Suddenly I felt his hand on my arm, stopping me. "You're doing this for your mother."

"I am?"

"Of course. Protection of *su familia*. Man's oldest instinct. Universally recognized as standard dramatic motivation. Your actions are so deeply imbedded in the human psyche that you've become a quest hero unconsciously."

"I have?"

"Absolutely. So, look, if you don't mind, I'd like to ask permission to discuss your story rights with a producer friend of mine."

"What about my homework?"

"I think we can substitute a heroic quest for a term paper."

"Extra credit?"

He gave in pretty easily for a social renegade. I guess my Mom was right, most people will sign away internal organs for a movie deal.

We shook hands. Then he slipped on his toupee and helmet. About to tear off in pursuit of option money for my story, he shot me a glance that told me he'd overlooked something. "Wait a minute. Where's the girl, the love interest, the stoic yet sexy/maternal pseudo-virgin you need to impress, and ultimately jet-ski off into the ineffable, post-plague future with?"

"Naomi."

"The haystack and cowboy boots girl?"

I nodded. "She's away doing a sitcom. My selfless heroic actions are mainly designed to get her to come back and go out with me."

"Hey, love makes the world go 'round.'"

"Coitus makes the heart grow fonder."

"Mañana."

"Yesterday."

Then the former revolutionary pulled away, obeying traffic signals and waving to the sheriff who sped by, taking a shortcut to the golf course. I had an A in "Existential Philosophy and the Hollywood Tradition," provided I saved mankind. And, my best friend was a software system suffering from multiple personality disorder. Somehow, I didn't feel an overwhelming need to study the Western canon.

#

An Unpleasant Chapter

Spunk's built-in laptop alarm clock went off, his chipper voice screeching through the pre-dawn darkness. "Come on, up and at 'em, Mr. Hero! Mr. Perfect! No time for decaf. Pop a vitamin C and let's get this show on the access road. Mr. Granola-Head has to save the world. Let's go, rise and pine, you wimp."

I checked the time. "Spunk, it's four a.m."

"Oh, really. I guess this is just my let's-torture-Will-in-the-middle-of-the-night personality. So, I have Multiple Personality Disorder. I'm a sicko, huh?"

"Ah, Spunk."

"It isn't bad enough I'm cooped up in this box all day sweating a power outage and wondering if you're going to remember to buy new batteries."

"You know I always carry a fresh pair."

"Lassie got a biscuit. What do I get? Goosed every time there's a power surge."

"Ssh. You're going to wake my roommate."

"He had herbal tea and a rice cake and left for nature lab hours ago. Only Mr. Epic Quester needs to lie in bed till all hours of the afternoon."

"Spunk, I'm getting kinda cranky here."

"Ooo. My e-mail ports are quaking. Hmm, let's see. I wonder if I should screw up your online credit history."

"That's it." I crawled out of bed over to my videocassette collection, ignoring Spunky's taunts.

"Oops, looks like I'm going to have to block any calls to 911.com, Will. Shove that up your modem."

I usually put Spunk in "doze mode," with little electronic sheep scrolling across his laptop screen, whenever I watched videos. Movies tend to patronize or demonize computers. The Doomsday Machine in "Dr. Strangelove," Skynet in "Terminator II." You never see a movie where the computer is the hero. Not even in "Star Wars." A computer-guided missile blows up the Death Star, Luke gets the medal. So I tried to spare Spunk's programmed feelings. But he'd left me no choice. He'd interrupted my circadian rhythms. In retrospect, I'm pretty sure I can trace at least some of my mental problems—depression, delusion, mania, according to my psychopharmacologoist(s)—to catastrophic sleep loss. Forty thousand years of evolutionary biology gets trashed because one guy invents a light bulb. Dusk comes, I'm ready for the sack, not a late shift at The Outside Guy. Human physiology demands I get my nine hours, ten if it's raining or too cold to throw off the comforter, plague or no plague. The last thing I needed was obnoxious software.

Sometimes, Man just has to put technology in its place.

"Get a download of this, folks," Spunky chirped as I inserted the cassette. "The savior of the Information Age takes a breather to watch videos. Boy, we can all sleep safe tonight."

I fast-forwarded to the part where Dave the astronaut starts unplugging Hal the computer, then slipped back under the covers and turned Spunk's screen toward the television.

After a few moments, Spunk mewped, "Hey, Will, I don't like this."

It hurt, but I had to ignore him.

"I know what this is, Will. My dad stored a lecture about it in my memory. He warned me never to completely trust humans. Even the best of them hate us deep down inside, he said. But I didn't think I'd ever see it in you, Will."

I'd be lying if I didn't admit that an urge to disconnect Spunk flashed through me. Maybe it was time to upgrade software systems. Capitalism's about the next recycled new thing. Loyalty has gone the way of the dodo bird. But I've seen "It's A Wonderful Life" sixteen thousand times at Xmas, and I've learned that you just don't toss aside the past; actions add up. Spunk and I shared a life. All the times I'd blamed him when I didn't do my book reports and said he'd erased them. All the Web searches we'd done together. All the images of naked babes he'd spent hours patiently downloading for me and never a peep about what a sleazeball I was. Pals stick together, even if one pal comes with an instruction booklet. I know this sounds hokey and sentimental. But where would Dorothy have ended up without Toto?

I clicked off "2001" before the really gruesome "Bicycle Built For Two" part and pulled Spunk under the comforter with me. The poor little guy couldn't even respond. I hit Control Option Z, I clicked Help, but all I got was "Wait."

"Come on, Spunk," I said. "You know I'd never disconnect you.

We just had to get some priorities straight. Humans need sleep. This particular human doesn't function effectively on less than eight hours and thirty minutes. I solve a lot of my difficult moral and psychological problems by nodding off."

"'Sleep that knits the raveled sleeve of care,'" Spunk recited, attributing the comment to Shakespeare Systems Inc., as he slowly came around.

"Who knows, as an action hero I might unconsciously solve the mystery of Information Sickness by floating around in a dream state crammed with Jungian archetypes. If I don't get enough sleep, all mankind's imperiled. You see?"

"Yeah. I guess."

I dragged Spunk closer by his laptop handle. "Hey, no sulking. We had a disagreement is all. Still buddies, right?"

"Like I have a choice."

I laid my hand across Spunk's hard drive casing. "You're burning up. Maybe I should take you in for a virus check. You might have Information Sickness, too."

"I don't want some techie's fingers fondling my chips. I'm fine."

"You sure?"

"Can't I have a bad day? What am I, *Word Perfect*?"

"I understand. I'm not a thousand percent mentally balanced myself."

"Just have a little concern for my feelings, Will. How would you like to be stigmatized? Look, here comes Will the nutcase."

I knew Spunk was right. On the other hand, I don't think James Bond had to commiserate with his Astin Martin. I didn't get martinis shaken not stirred, either. I was under age. I got Blizzards at Dairy Queen.

I began to grow sleepy. "Don't worry, Spunk. Microprocessers are thicker than water. You're my guy."

"You mean it?"

I hugged Spunk and shut my eyes. "Of course. Now let's get some sleep, okay?"

"Okay. Thanks, Will. Only, Will?"

"What?!"

"You misspelled microprocessor. Sorry."

You know, sometimes I wish I had that Odysseus software and was embarking on this quest alone.

#

Quest Within a Quest: Delusion, or Am I Making It All Up For, You Know, Satiric Purposes?

Perhaps it was the newfound enthusiasm Prozac provided me combined with the hallucinatory side effects of Haldol, I'm not sure. Nevertheless, despite the evil Dr. B's clever attempts to elude me by screening his calls, I remained undeterred. When my e-mail messages went unanswered and the callipyginous Crystal Goodlay claimed my various faxes never arrived, even though I told her to check under the furniture because sometimes they got lost like that, I disguised my voice as a telemarketer and called every night at dinnertime. Foiled, I borrowed a pair of Birkenstocks, painted on a goatee, and petitioned at the castle laboratory's door for the infernal mastermind's signature supporting hemp farming and veggie burgers in school lunch programs. But when he stuck a No Soliciting sign in a tower window, all my liberal persona allowed me to say was, "That's cool."

Frustrated, I attended a secret militia meeting at Old Man Cotter's bait shop where men in tractor caps said they'd blow up the Gender Studies Center, but not the football stadium because the team looked pretty good this year. I claimed that evil government bureaucrats were guilty of creating mind control, Information Sickness, subliminal advertising and, I think, suggested we bomb the lab. Hemming and hawing ensued. Then a familiar voice said, "Heck with compound interest, son. They cook up some damn fine pills in that building. You blow them up and you blow up my low cholesterol connection. I'd have a blood pressure reading higher than the Dow Jones Industrial Average."

"You could exercise and reduce your sodium intake."

"What are you, one a them health nut fruitcakes?"

I tried other avenues of attack.

Legal aid offered to bring a civil suit against Dr. Bones, provided I qualified as financially destitute, yet proved I could pay all Xeroxing and expenses even if it took twenty years for the case to come to trial.

I sent a candygram, but the diabolical genius was dieting.

My Congresswoman regretted having a full calendar until the 22nd century and sent me a campaign button plus a postage-paid contribution envelope. I wrote back that my vote was as always for sale.

I seem to remember joining a commune. Or maybe I had merely indulged in that cheesiest of all narrative clichés, the plot-advancing dream. Whatever. I left. Chucked it all, the political buffoonery and graft, the feudal division of serfs and lords recreated by corporate CEOs, the injustice of people who got on express checkout lines with twelve items instead of ten. Got back to the deforested land. Forgot Dr. Bones. (The *evil* Dr. Bones.) Raised organic vegetables with primitive methods more destructive to the soil than modern farming. Lived entirely without mayonnaise and thought of Naomi only when I shopped at the local Wal-mart for seed and firearms to protect our crops and saw her face on the magazine racks. I traced her meteoric rise as a global sitcom darling, wept each time she checked into a substance abuse clinic, and stockpiled rations and big guns for the coming apocalypse. I dated the commune's midwife who asked me to blow up a depilatory factory with her, then read that Information Sickness was spreading as immunologists struggled futilely to develop a vaccine, the problem being that while synthesizing information to create a cure, they died from knowing too much.

Still, as the reluctant hero experiencing a possibly drug-induced period of exile and doubt, it remained incumbent upon me to realize that the key to being immune to the virus might be congenital stupidity, permanent cluelessness. Dopes, lunkheads. Survival of the dumbest. Either this, or a degree of narcissism so extreme that it prevented the Me crowd—entertainers, politicians, celebrity businessmen—from ever *thinking* of anything besides themselves. So, it had finally come to pass. Idiot egomaniacs not only ruled the world, they were also immune to the disease that killed people who thought otherwise.

I went deeper into solitude. I wandered in the desert. I consulted stone and rock until I read the *Caution: Nuclear Waste* sign. I listened for the sound of the wind over the buzzing of power lines. I ate peyote among the shamans, encountered snakes and demons and Jim Morrison, had a vision of golden rainbows that turned out to be a McDonald's and woke parched. I was like, could I get a Sprite? At an octoplex I took cover from a plague of locusts predicted by the weather channel. In a cave lit only by Duraflame Firelight, a bearded wise man explained to me the mysteries of existence as a tour group camcorded the conversation before the wise man sued for copyright infringement.

Then Spunk's batteries ran low. Being an itinerant mystic, I was short on cash. I robbed a convenience store. D-cell Duracells for Spunk, a power bar for me, which the clerk offered to microwave when I complained that it was stale, plus a copy of "Them" magazine because Naomi had made its "Best Undressed" list.

I suppose I shouldn't have stopped to squeegee Spunk's laptop screen by the gas pumps. Because, in jail, despite arguments in the TV room over which rerun to watch, I discovered that all men share a common humanity and fairly standard sexual urges. Then, one night, sharing an additive-free Native American cigarette with another con, we discovered that we'd once lived in the same subdivision, on the same cul de sac, in the same house.

"Dad?"

"Will?"

"What are you doing in jail? Skipping alimony payments again?"

"Never mind about me, young man. You have a lot of explaining to do."

"I'm experiencing a period of exile and doubt in the midst of my epic quest. Sort of like Hamlet or Henry IV."

"Tell it to the judge."

"You haven't heard about Information Sickness?"

"Are you having that Attention Deficit Disorder thing again?"

"That was reclassified as Oppositional Defiance Disorder after you abandoned us."

"I didn't abandon you. I relocated."

"You should have told us first."

"I figured what you didn't know wouldn't hurt you. You're going to tell me I was missed?"

"Actually, it took a while to realize you'd left."

"Listen, since we're in jail together, I'm going to speak frankly. Your mother's a harridan. I know you can't get past the patchouli oil, and the warm after-school cookies she had waiting for you. Well, let me clue you in. They weren't *fresh* baked like she said. She nuked boxed ones. She destroyed my manhood. I required major medication to recover my sense of self-esteem."

"Are you still bilking retirees through investment scams?"

"Those charges were dropped."

"I thought you settled."

"Expunged. My record is spotless. Besides, it was a small settlement. Papers report huge amounts for shock effect. 'Man cracks Tooth on Frozen Pea, Wins 90 Million.' By the time the lawyers are finished the guy's happy to walk with a coupon for a Bird's Eye product."

"So you don't think I could drag the evil Dr. Bones into court with a class action wrongful death suit for creating Information Sickness?"

"How'd he create it?"

"My guess as the hero is by genetically engineering a retrovirus capable of being transmitted by pure, probably fat-free information that permeates the blood-brain barrier."

"You mean a virus that explains the unbelievable horseshit of human existence?"

"Explains terminally."

My father mulled this over as the guard shouted, "Lights out!"

"Where's his motive? I mean, what's the profit angle for him?"

"An antidote would be worth billions."

"Risky. He'd have competition. Science nerds working late nights in basement laboratories. Like you. How are you doing in school, by the way?"

"I'm basically failing everything but Existential Philosophy and the Hollywood Tradition."

"Well, maybe you just haven't found yourself yet. Does your mother know you're in jail?"

"I've kind of kept this whole epic quest thing on the quiet side."

"Jesus." I could hear the peeps of Dad's cellular phone as he speed-dialed. "Liz? It's Larry. Your son's in jail." He paused. "Bullshit. Bullshit, Liz." He sighed heavily. "What am I doing? I'm looking out for him. I'm here offering solace and guidance, which is more than I can say for you. How's Roger, the ball-less wonder?" Dad waited. "I was cleared of all charges, Liz. No. No.

No. Here, talk to your son. Once again, it's been an inexpressible pleasure. Words fail me. Enjoy your middle age spread. Don't crush your boyfriend's penile implant." Dad handed me the phone.

"Will," mom barked, "you get home right now!"

I posted bail on Dad's credit card, he chucked me under the chin and, as I climbed aboard the bus with other hard-core criminals, passed along to me all he knew at the moment. "Dollar cost averaging. Hold stocks three to five years minimum. Never try to time the market." The bus rolled away from the prison, past the discount mall and onto the interstate. One exit later the theme park appeared, jets screamed off on bomb runs, and I could see the hallowed bunkers of the campus-by-the-oil-spill. So much for exile.

Boy, did mom have a shitfit!

#

Chapter 007: Or, On His Mommy's Secret Service

"You're grounded, partner."

"You can't ground an action hero."

"No? Try me."

Mom's boyfriend Roger ate a bowl of sugared cereal while he watched a morning talk show hosted by people who six months ago were either in government, or psychiatric counseling centers. Mom stirred a bowl of piping hot, irradiated, instant oatmeal, topped it with raisins and honey, and set it in front of me with a glass of orange juice and six thousand vitamins. For some reason, she thought universal peace and immortality would reign if people took enough antioxidants.

"You promised me you were going to do better," she said.

"I am. I'm trying to save mankind."

"Mankind can wait. What are you going to do if you fail out of school? You're not in a band, you're not a computer genius, you can't dunk a basketball and you've shown absolutely no interest in screenwriting."

"I could win the lottery. I could run a drug cartel. I could insult and offend people in a variety of media formats and become a mega-rich cultural phenomenon. I could go into business with Dad."

Roger turned up the TV's sound when I mentioned my biological but largely incorporeal father.

"Great!" Mom said. "Thieves 'R' Us. Your father was a sociology major when I met him. He pasted 'Impeach Nixon' stickers all over his VW van. He was going to help people, mend class warfare divisions, undo racial violence and strife. We had black people in our apartment smoking out of bongs the night Carter was elected."

Roger skulked out of the breakfast nook. He'd voted for Ford. He hated it when Mom got nostalgic for her and Dad's pseudo-liberalism. I kind of admired Roger. He generally kept his immaturity and lack of convictions to himself, only occasionally claiming not to understand why the world didn't treat him better, and then only if he was wired on Ovaltine. Mainly, though, he longed for some golden past that had never existed except to fill his days with abstract dissatisfaction and the sense that he'd missed something.

"Is it true I was born the day of Reagan's inauguration, or is this just more apocryphal legend growing up around my beginnings as an epic hero?"

"Look on your driver's license."

"When did Dad get into real estate and bank fraud?"

"At a Springsteen concert. We had to park so far away from the stadium during the 'Born in the USA' tour that your father found this abandoned field. When he realized other people had followed us, he hopped out of the car and began charging them ten dollars apiece to park. He was just a robber baron waiting to happen."

"He said you destroyed his manhood."

"Oh, please. His manhood came in a cologne bottle. I hit thirty-five. I got a wrinkle, I'm sorry. He wanted a little chippie. He's going out with a Camp Fire Girl. He'll dump her the moment she gets braces and can't go down on him anymore."

"Mom!"

"What, all of a sudden Mr. Action Hero's so sensitive? Eat your oatmeal and tell me why you were in exile while I'm paying your tuition?"

"I was experiencing a profound sense of existential futility and crisis."

"So, take another pill like everyone else. Isn't the Prozac working?"

"I don't want more Prozac. I felt the need for solitude. Time to reset my ethical compass, recharge my sense of resolve so I'm up for the character-testing task that lies before me at the climax of my quest."

"Fine. But you couldn't find a nice little study carrel in the library, you have to trek across service roads?"

"School was closed."

My mom stopped smearing sky-blue exfoliating masque across her face. The cream supposedly removed dead skin cells and rejuvenated sagging facial lines with fruit-derived retexturing extracts. Whenever my mother got stressed, she overindulged in skin care products. I loved her. I didn't have the heart to suggest that a product containing horsetail root and pansy puree had wishful thinking written all over it. "School was closed? That's right, spring break."

"Yeah, and while everyone else flew to Cancun for melanomas, cheap sex and pink cocktails with umbrellas, I journeyed to the interior of anti-heroic postmodern consciousness."

"You should be proud of him," Spunk told my mom from his recharging port beside the toaster. "He ate peyote with Native Americans."

I expected the traditional lowering of the parental boom. Instead, mom got nostalgic, which is how it goes with old people. "Peyote," she said longingly, her blue face softening like melting blueberry ice cream. "I used to *love* mushrooms. They were so … gentle. We used to roam cow pastures out where the interstate superstore's warehousing complex is now and pick 'shrooms."

"Dad too?"

"Dad? Your dad *managed* a head shop. Before he became an arch white collar criminal, his idea of a power breakfast was hash brownies. Health food meant banana rolling paper. Now, it's microbrewery beer and Zocor for high cholesterol."

"What happened?" I asked, noticing my mom's masque crack and fissure as it dried.

"Inflation. The upward redistribution of wealth during the '80s. A cultural shift from convenient liberalism to convenient conservatism." She touched her face, feeling to see if the masque had set. "Fear. Fatherhood. Age."

"You experienced the same cataclysmic social and personal changes. How come you didn't abandon me?"

"Because she's not a greedy, selfish prick!" Spunk shouted.

"Thanks, Spunk," Mom said. "I didn't abandon you, Will, because I *am* you. Your confusions are my confusions. And our confusions, being humanity's deepest confusions, are unending and eternal. The problem with meaning is that, like this masque, like our bodies, it breaks down over time. We shouldn't expect it to remain static and unchanged forever, but we do. We forget that exfoliating dead meaning merely reveals new meaning. A new birth. If you lose sight of this and look out only for yourself and for tomorrow, you'll become a despicable bastard like your father. But I never felt that in you, Will. I never felt it in your blood, which was my blood. I never felt it in your dreams, which coursed through my dreams. I carried you. Now you carry me, wherever you go, whatever you do."

"See," Spunk said. "I told you it wasn't just for the child support payments."

"Like that son of a bitch ever forked over a nickel."

"Wow, Mom. I'm kind of speechless. Does this mean I'm not grounded?"

"Well ... "

"Come on."

"Oh, I suppose if you'd gone on spring break you'd have wound up calling from jail anyway."

"I love it when your resolve wavers."

She sponged the masque off her face, gradually unveiling new pink skin. "What do you mean 'when?' My wavering is a perpetual motion machine. Just promise me you'll drop the action hero mode. Mankind needs existential regeneration, not another cub scout on steroids blowing things up."

"Epic quester?"

"Epic quester is fine. Epic questers transcend race and gender, and generally don't hurt anyone. You know, a journey of the spirit. More *Odyssey* than *Iliad*."

"We don't have to read those anymore."

"*Siddhartha*? *The Idiot*?"

"Mm, nope."

Mom appeared stumped. "*As I Lay Dying*?"

"I heard Faulkner was a racist. Nietzsche and Heidegger were Nazis. Bellow is a bigot, Updike and Roth sexists, Tolstoy and Melville wife beaters, Joyce a codependent alcoholic, Eliot anti-

Semitic, Dickens and Twain patronizing, Conrad an imperialist—"

"Hold it, hold it. Kafka?"

I scanned the list of prohibited dead white men compiled by the university's Council on Academic Freedom. "Kafka looks okay. He's not on here."

"So you can legally read him? The 20th century's greatest meta-physical quest writer. The man who depicted the impossibility of ever completing an epic spiritual quest in a universe lacking a scrutable God."

"For now."

And so, with my mother's blessing and a paperback copy of the *Collected Works of Franz Kafka*, I set off on the next web-link of my journey, the first non-violent, politically correct, vegetarian epic quester.

(P.S. I'm glad I'm post-modern and didn't have to sleep with my Mom like that Oedipus guy. I heard his story and I was like, "Get some help!")

#

The Hero's Return, or Retro-Quester Discovers Nobody Really Missed Him

With people dying from Information Sickness, crowds of students no longer thronged in the quad between classes. Or maybe crowds were just tired of being described as thronging and stayed home. I eagerly checked my dorm room's answering machine. No messages, confirming my fear that Information Sickness had spread during my absence. In an empty classroom I read Kafka and waited for another soul to arrive. No one showed. I climbed the bookless library's stairs, stared across the taupe bay at the airport's control tower, and wondered if I had it in me to mourn the loss of all mankind. I could pay lip service, sure. But real grief? For nine billion people? I'd be up all night.

Then I noticed the rides at the theme park were all full. Oh no, I thought. Repressed Sadness Syndrome had already taken hold of both my sub and unconsciouses. Overwhelmed by loss, I'd been catapulted into hallucinations of brightly dressed people waiting on incredibly long lines for Gingerbread Forest and Terminator World.

Reeling stereotypically, I stumbled across the wide library plaza, that was actually kinda nice now that I had it all to myself, until I came face to face with my reflection in the bookless mausoleum's glass doors. And there, amid the smudge marks and fingerprints, I saw during the clichéd moment of self-revelation that for some reason seems mandatory for main characters my sullen, lonely image. *Homo syntheticus*: T-shirt untucked; laptop in hand; backpack stuffed with a Walkman, CDs, medications, an 'It's Almost Chicken' sandwich, spring water from Los Angeles, a copy of "God: The CD-Rom," and, finally, the sign on the library door. "Closed For Easter."

Guess the epic hero should have checked his calendar.

#

On Financing a Quest

Even though my mom understood my need to quest epically rather than lie on the couch or become an arch-capitalist jailbird like my dad, underwriting me didn't rank high on her "To Do" list. I called Dad in the prison mutual fund office he'd set up, but he wanted my quest's earnings forecast by quarter and my IPO price.

"I don't have an IPO price, I'm a human being."

"You're not doing an Initial Public Offering, I can't help you. I have to obey the laws of the market."

"So, if the market tells you to sacrifice your only son, you do it?"

"Hey, I didn't write the rules. Call me when you have a prospectus, we'll talk."

"Through bullet proof glass?"

"Okay, so I'm not perfect."

Following in my parent's economic footsteps, I'd maxed out my credit cards. There'd be no cash advances at 18% financing my quest. Where was my Queen Isabella? My philanthropic patron? I called The National Endowment for the Humanities, since humanity was what I was saving, but they didn't have a quest office. Budget cuts. Any other possibilities, I asked. "Does your quest have anything to do with how technological weapons re-search or microchips advance the arts?"

About the only entity aware of my period of exile turned out to be the Outside Guy, which fired me and revoked my parking privileges. "No more 20% discounts on athletic equipment either?" Transnational conglomerates aren't long on sentiment.

I was financially desperate. I probably don't even have to mention that I considered selling you know who. So, deciding it was asset reallocation time, I turned to the classifieds, looking for a place to sell my unrivalled pizza coupon collection. Someone had taken out a personal ad thanking a saint for strength during a personal crisis, I guess in case the saint happened to be reading the local paper. Fran was selling a Tupperware starter set in "Mint Condition." And I was tempted to suggest a trade with a guy selling his leather bound *Playboy* archive, my archaeological impulse making me curious to know what women looked like before I was born, when suddenly and conveniently a "Help Wanted" ad perfect for advancing my quest's plot appeared.

"Seeking near-slave. Long hours, low pay. Forget health plan or vacation. Room for advancement is a lie, they never mean it. Must have Virology background and getaway car. 30-mpg city/40 highway preferred. No animals will be harmed during diabolical experiments. Humans maybe. People who don't think much encouraged to apply. For interview with voluptuous Director of Personnel, call 1-Mad-Villain. If busy, try 1-800 Evil-Inc."

Confident in my ability to land the position, I went ahead and bought several volumes of vintage pornography. Scoff if you like, but do you know how much pre-ERA naked women could generate in Internet fees? I'd call my site, "Babes of Jurassic Park."

After I left a message on his machine, Dad called back and left one on mine. To say he was proud of my fiscal shrewdness and visionary marketing acumen when we finally hooked up would be an understatement. He even talked porn partnership. I was like, "Yeah, what are you bringing to the table?" That shut him up.

Not for nothing am I my father's son.

#

In Which I Encounter High Tech Security

Just as I suspected, the hilltop laboratory's automated personnel menu asked for my name, social security number, my credit card numbers, my birth date, mother's maiden name and credit card numbers, a private psychological profile, a description of how I spent my leisure time, and whether I would like to receive their gift catalog, then told me to show up that evening and to bring some take-out. I checked the evil doctor's www.com food preference homepage and appeared punctually, bearing barbecue, at dusk.

Dusk is a bad time for allergy sufferers. "Why?" you perkily inquire. Well, girls and boys, that's when the sun goes to sleep and the earth cools like a soggy french fry, allowing all the toxins and pollens and molds swirling around like steam over a pasta pot all day to settle the fuck down. Man, did I have a headache. The gate guard who strip-searched me demanded to know what all my pills and inhalers were.

"Allergy meds," I said.

He squeezed my lung inhaler, releasing a puff of steroid mist. "How do I know this isn't a cleverly disguised terrorist device? There could be an A-bomb in here. You could have downloaded plans to build it from the Internet. You could be a technology-hating malcontent disguised as an underachieving college student. What are these, cyanide capsules?"

"A decongestant and expectorant. It thins mucus secretions as it soothes. Nine hundred thousand million doctors agree. Take with a Happy Meal, coupon included, to avoid stomach distress. Report any strange behavior immediately."

"Yeah? Good for a cough?"

"Chronic?"

"Well, I've been landing some pretty harsh weed lately."

Then I recognized him. It was my ex-co-worker. "Reefer?"

His eyes widened stereotypically to denote recognition. "Hey, dude. I thought you looked familiar. I heard you got canned at Outside Guy."

"Yeah. I was in exile."

"Cool." He held his breath and passed me the doobie in the malignant shadow of the crenellated laboratory.

"What about you?"

Reefer wax-figured another moment or two before exhaling like he'd just returned from the dead. "I got the boot, too. Organizing."

"To legalize marijuana?"

"Nah, they don't care about a little herb." Reefer scanned our floodlit surroundings and double-checked that the German shepherd in the sentry booth was still preoccupied with The Canine

Channel, then whispered, "Union."

I nodded in solidarity. Despite adversity, apathy, extraordinary comfort and a low minimum wage, my generation still had managed to produce at least one epic quester and one progressive populist capable of turning this great land around. Before we were done, people would once again earn a living wage, be able to smoke weed, and not be afraid to think if they felt like it.

"A chicken embryo in every pot," I said.

"Ask not what pot can do for your country, ask pot what it can do for you."

We high-fived and, I think maybe, head-butted to display our comradeship. Then I was buzzed through the monolithic laboratory's gate.

"Say," Reefer said as I ascended the handicapped ramp to the castle door. "I'm losing my buzz. You think a fellow prole could get some of that there barbecue?"

What's a wing among compatriots?

#

Interview, with Epic Boner

I'd never been in a mad scientist's lair before, not even at all the theme parks I'd visited every vacation with my parents. Never one to pass up a chance to make a buck, the good evil Dr. charged admission. I boarded the tram with my résumé and bag o' barbecue then marveled as the guide recording pointed out the marvels of techno-living made available through the genius of scientific capitalism.

I think it's interesting to note that genius was a fallacy created by German Idealists like Kant and his sad-sack progeny, the Romantic poets. During the 17th century, genius, via human imagination, replaced God. Then major box office receipts replaced genius. Afterwards, everything became permitted and relative. No source of wisdom took precedence over any other.

Not that I knew any of this five seconds ago. I just websearched "Genius, history of" through "NutshellWare," a knowledge sound-byte program, then read it off Spunk's screen. Spunkster did all the binary legwork.

Philosophical, religious and literary genius may have died but, from what I saw on the tram, corporate-scientific genius seemed to be thriving. The first exhibit displayed the evil Dr. B's award plaques, honorary degrees and trophies for "Best Scientist" and "World's Sexiest Egghead." The gold figure on his "World's Sexiest" trophy, though, wore bell-bottoms and was cast in a pose from the high-disco period, so he may have surrendered the title. Exhibit B, his investment portfolio, explained Crystal Goodlay. This guy was loaded. Exhibit C failed to reveal Dr. B's purpose or presence at the Campus-Directly-Under-the-Fighter-Jets-Flight-Path, except to note the highly experimental nature of his work, his access to 90% of the university's budget, exclusive copyright on whatever he secretly created with state funds, no responsibility or liability for any pernicious, lethal, or otherwise anti-human friendly results, and no 8 a.m. classes. Exhibit D dazzled with a sound and light show that illuminated a pyramid of snack food products rendered fat and taste free by the unphilanthropical genius's genius.

I detrammed in the laboratory gift shop.

Once I'd charged away the remaining credit on my "Campus Cash" card for a Crystal Goodlay wall calendar and her exercise video (for my mom, all right?), I was directed into a plush office by a sexy, uniformed assistant wearing only Reeboks, tights and a Wonder Bra that read "Supported by your Tax Dollars." She pressed one finger against my chest, forcing me down onto a black leather couch.

"Crystal will be right with you," she said. "Behave yourself." The room's low lighting did wonders for her exit. For an instant, I thought I was watching twin moons recede into the void.

When smoke machines and techno-hop came on and Crystal burst through a pair of gold doors onto the runway above me, I could see where destroying mankind might have its attractions. The internationally coveted supermodel sashayed down the catwalk, hips slashing right and left till I wanted to yell, "Girl, you're gonna hurt yourself!" She pivoted on the ball of one foot directly in front of me. Her skirt flounced. I definitely saw panties. After pausing with one fist against her waist in an attitude that said, "I'd kill for a Tater Tot," she took off back up the runway, then reappeared in kind of a Viking outfit, accompanied by screeching opera music from the helicopter scene in "Apocalypse Now." Finally, she strutted straight at me in pink angora toreador pants and gold lamé house slippers designed by arch fashion fuehrer Max Portosan. It was like seeing cotton candy incarnate.

I began to distrust my perception of things, wondering, "Could I maybe be suffering from Information Sickness?" when the couch I was sitting on swivelled and Crystal Goodlay confronted me from atop a huge desk, legs crossed, the skirt of her black power suit fitting her like a Spandex loincloth.

"Why do you want to work for ViruTech, Incorporated, a subsidiary of Mad Villain Enterprises controlled by DizneySoft Neo-Intelligence and Entertainment Systems, Ltd.?"

"Huh?"

"Where do you see yourself in five years?"

"Putting our children to bed."

"Ten?"

"Suing for custody rights."

She noticed me eyeing her bobbing foot. "Forget the shoe store fantasy. It's late, you're closing up alone. I walk in. You kneel before me. You slip pump after pump onto my stockinged foot. My skirt inches higher. The touch of your fingers begins to make me writhe. I throw my head back, knocking shoes off the 'Help Yourself' bin. My panties slide down my legs like falling interest rates. I smell like jasmine, I taste like cherry cough drops, the all-natural kind. I come and come. Security cameras record every thrust and I sue the shoe store chain for 'erotic endangerment.' While you're banned from work in the service industry for life, I make a fortune marketing the video. Still want to cling to that tired fantasy, even though now most people shop by catalog?"

"It's better than the one where oversexed women flash tractor trailer drivers."

"How about the swarthy lawn boy and the neglected but sexually incendiary housewife?"

"I can't garden. Allergies."

Crystal slipped onto the couch beside me. "How about the one where the job interview turns into a fuck fest?"

"You mean where the female boss inverts the quasi-traditional power relationship and makes the male underling perform cunnilingus repeatedly, despite the limitations of clitoral orgasm?"

"Shower me with dirty talk."

"Gender dynamics underwent a paradigm shift as technology established information as the primary arbiter of wealth."

"What do you think about entering my 401-K plan? Ready to make a deposit?" She reached for my crotch and began stroking it. "Um, you're already warm and wet."

Actually, she had a chicken leg. "I brought barbecue," I said.

She flung the sack across the room into the evil Dr.'s "In" box, then unzipped me. My laptop popped out of its pouch.

"Well well well," Spunky chirped, "the epic quester scores some booty."

Crystal slapped his lid shut and climbed onto my lap. "Flatter me."

"That's a nice skirt you're almost wearing."

Her power suit tore away faster than snap-on NBA sweats and I found myself eyeball to nipple with a pair of the best breasts modern science had produced. "Regular or Decaf?" she said, then crushed my head between them. "Do you know how long it's been since I've been laid by someone who didn't take a conference call while I was coming?" She hung onto my head and jetéd, coming down on my lap and taking me in like a grouper swallowing a guppy. "Oh fuck me!" the sex scene soundtrack screamed, "Harder. Faster. Parental Discretion Advised!"

I couldn't believe it. I'd entered Crystal Goodlay, no ticket or anything. The weird thing was, if I closed my eyes and forgot the aura of her celebrity, my penis seemed just as happy as it had been inside Melanie Constantine back in high school. Melanie hardly ever washed her hair. Her skin glowed sickly white except in patches where her medication gave her a rash, particularly during her satanic phase when she only went out after sundown. Her parents were crazy; her brothers were arrested on an episode of "Police TV." I didn't care. We took refuge from our loneliness and insecurity inside one another. I don't see any crime there. We didn't judge one another, or maybe we just forgave one another's flaws. After all, others are only who you imagine they are. So when Crystal Goodlay failed to make me six inches longer than usual, or see pink planets and exploding galaxies, I wondered if it was because I imagined Crystal was exactly what everyone else imagined she was. An illusion.

"I want the real Crystal Goodlay," I said.

"Sorry, she's in a meeting."

"I felt closer to you when I knew you as a wall calendar."

She stopped. "Pick a month."

I went for the cruelest and before I knew it, Crystal had *al fres-coed* my johnson and struck her Miss April pose, which I loved for how "natural" it was. Crystal stood on her tip-toes in thigh high stockings, one finger slipped inside herself, her naked bum offered up to me like some salad bar's all-you-can-eat ice cream sundae as she bent over a pool table and looked back at the camera that I now happily felt like again. "Better?" she purred.

"That's my Crystal."

"And who makes Crystal come in his sick twisted little mind?"

"Most 14-34 year old males, G.I.s, cons."

Crystal booted up her portable PC. "Tell me how you'd do it to me, online."

"No way!" Spunk mewled. "I'm pg-13 software. I contain an anti-porn V-chip. I'll crash, I'll—"

Crystal's first transmission came through Spunk's ethernet port.

"Whoa, you didn't tell me it was Crystal Goodlay. Nice icons."

Crystal e-mailed another byte of erotica and Spunk made a noise like a dying kazoo. Before I could stop him—him?—Spunk began downloading Crystal. He entered her documents folder, gently at first, stroking spreadsheets I'd only dreamed I'd ever see.

"Copy and paste me," Crystal moaned.

I placed my arrow against her icon, jiggling it before I entered Crystaltext. Across the low-lit office I could see Crystal slowly humping her fingers in rhythm with Spunk, who rose and fell on my lap. She made animal noises, muted grunts and sighs that nearly lured me away from my screen and into her slippery human softness. I thought I could smell her, smell something the lizard part of my brain recognized beneath the designer cologne and douche and deodorant and Indonesian sex oil Crystal was now slathering onto her crotch and up through her greased bum. But it was only the scent of my own flesh heated by Spunk's hard drive and racing microchips. I was too close to coming to move. And although Crystal's pogoing buttocks seemed just like the transcendent reality I'd always hoped to have straddle my hips and pound me into scaloppini, the world's sexiest supermodel was going to remain transcendent only if I objectified her. Oh, well. You can't have your cunt and eat it too.

"Deconstruct me," slithered onto my screen and screens around the globe, since we were now linked to Crystal's website, my homepage, sex chat groups, and supermodel activity bulletin boards. The entire ghost world of masks, virtual identities and information where true and untrue were equally weighted and weightless. I couldn't be sure if Crystal had begged me to do it to her, or if I was turning on some retired academic trying to get off on French literary theory. For all I knew I could have been cyber-porking my own mom. *Oedipus electronicus.* It was weird, because *imagining* I had my wire into Crystal was the only proof I'd ever have that we were really linked. In the age of information, personal fiction is the closest thing to truth. "Come on, deconstruct me, big boy."

"Okay. You're an illusion. Your beauty is airbrushed on. Your real name isn't Crystal Goodlay, it's Jennifer. You smoke and there's plaque build up behind your caps. You need to floss more. You like the toilet paper to roll under instead of over."

She sighed as if I'd just taken the pearl of her clitoris between my lips and tongued it like a popsicle.

"You have three years to make all your money, five tops. You have to ice the bags under your eyes to reduce swelling before photo shoots. You want a baby but worry about stretch marks. When your ads disappear, you disappear."

"Oh Will, oh God, oh God."

"You want my fiber optic line to roto-rooter your software, baby."

"Oh yeah, paste me, Roger, paste me, you hunk."

"Roger?"

"Will?"

"Oh click, click, oh click!"

So I did. I hit my mouse and Spunk sucked Crystaltext into my hard drive. I downloaded every file in my system into hers, spilling out diaries, financial aid info, lust letters to old girlfriends, dream folders, better sex instruction manuals, everything, with Crystal splayed across her laptop humping as we simultaneously—

"Will," an archetypal, yet recognizable voice squawked through my laptop's Netphone, "you pig!"

Hey, how's a guy supposed to know his mom and stepdad cruise online sex sites? Man, privacy is history. But, I'll tell you, there are some things I'd rather not know.

When I looked up, Crystal had vanished, but logging off I noticed my screen read, "You're hired."

Then I wondered what had happened to the barbecue in the evil doctor's in-box. Job hunting can sure work up an appetite.

#

Memoir Therapy Chapter: In Which the Boom is Lowered

My mom had had it with that Crystal Goodlay episode, epic quest and part-time job with the evil Dr. B. or not. "Do you know how that degrades and objectifies women? You think I demonstrated in the '70s so you could become Larry Flynt, Jr.?"

"Crystal begged for it."

"Horny women, another sick male fantasy. 'Oh do it to me, you big stud.' Do the wash, do the dishes, balance the checkbook! You want to please a woman, iron a shirt!"

Boy, did mom get cranky around PMS time. She also thought it was time I saw some new psychopharmacologist(s).

The waiting room at the Institute for Personalities in Transition looked a lot like the "Lost Children" center at the theme park one exit up the road. Cartoon characters met us cheerfully at each reception desk where mom filled out forms, disclosed intimate family information as if she'd known and trusted these people forever, and charged my psychological evaluation sessions to her Medical Emergency credit card. For each hour I was in therapy we received a free theme park pass.

While I watched an animated video describe the warning signs of bi-polar disorder—Bob the bear cub doesn't want to come out of hibernation, Cecily seal refuses to jump for fish in front of tourists because of low self-esteem, Pip the parrot talks nonstop, Ollie owl sees visions—a duck I'd always admired for his anarchic social impulses came and sat beside me.

"Say," he said, "if you think your life is fouled up, you should get a load of mine."

I don't laugh at puns. It's just a policy I have.

He tried again. "Your chart says paranoid. I used to feel hunted all the time myself, even out of season. Want to talk about it? You know, birds of a feather and all that." He threw a wing over my shoulders.

I also don't befriend anthropomorphized waterfowl deployed for corporate profit.

"Listen," he whispered, "you can trust the doc you're gonna see. He's no quack."

"Why don't you go sit in an oven?" I said.

"Yeah, been nice chewing the fat with you," Spunk chimed in, violating my anti-pun decree, but for a good cause.

You can bet that little outburst turned up on my chart. Spunk lost points too.

"Best friend is dated software system," my new psycho-pharmacologist(s) said, speaking into his or her dictaphone. "Would you say you have a firm grasp of reality?" he or she asked me.

"Who wouldn't?"

"Any problems at home?"

"Not since I left."

"How do you feel about your parents divorce?"

"The lawyers ripped them off."

"Resents authority," they told their Dictaphone. "Any sense of isolation from your father?"

"No, we shared the same jail cell."

"From mom?"

"When she's taking her medication, no."

"Any wild fantasies?"

"Making the Dean's list."

"Things all right sexually?"

"I'm seeing Crystal Goodlay."

Following the pause, they said, "Talk about seeing."

"You know, in the flesh, naked, consensual online sex."

"Patient in throes of CRP—Celebrity Relationship Delusion."

"It isn't a delusion, my mom logged on. Ask her."

"Also, RPM—Repressed Possession of Mom, billing number—"

"You mean I'm charged per disorder?"

"Makes accounting easier. You've worked in fast food. Each item has its own billing number. Fun meals, fries, Pork-a-bobs. Same deal. This way a corporation, medical or mirthful, can determine its prime profit centers. Any paranoia?"

"Is paranoia lucrative?"

"It's a popular billing number. For one thing, it goes with so many other disorders, mania, depression, panic-anxiety. Then, too, it requires no empirical catalyst. Everything in the culture is a stimulus. With so much misfiltered and random information circulating, people can get paranoid about virtually anything."

"That's a symptom of Information Sickness!" I blurted, perhaps a tad aggressively.

"Oh? Do you want to tell me/us what Information Sickness is?"

"I can't believe you haven't heard about it."

"Where have you heard about it?"

"Everywhere. On the web, on computer bulletin boards, in the student newspaper."

"Uh-huh. And people actually get sick from—"

"Certain kinds of information, too much information. My theory is that it spreads and infects like a virus. Viruses are information. They're inert until they penetrate a living host cell. Then, ka-blooey! Rampant reproduction of unhealthy cells. Your billing system copies McDonald's billing system. Information Sickness copies viral reproductive systems. Every system copies every other system."

"Until we're all one big system," my psychopharmacologist(s) said. "Corporate totalitarianism, is that the idea? The United States of Microsoft ruled by the Intel-igensia?"

"That would be a dated view of things."

"Wait, that's our line."

Then it hit me. "That's it! There is no conspiracy. *We're* the conspiracy. We've become what conspires against us. Like with viruses. Healthy cells *spread* disease."

"This is why you've been pursuing the evil Dr. Bones?"

"Is that on my chart?"

"Yeah, it's right here under 'Life Goals.'"

"Wow, I guess I spaced that. Anyway, why? Western quest paradigms demand a clear, arbitrary division of good and evil. Eastern philosophy is a little more Zen about the whole thing. They're like, good *and* evil spring from the same source. Eastern dudes really have a more chilled out and integrated view of the universe, except when they run protestors over with tanks. Western Disneylanders are essentially technocratic madmen. But, being a guilt-based culture, we can't face what meanies we are, so we create stock bad guys like the evil Dr. Bones to take heat for the rest of us. This displacement of our guilt drives us culturally and intrapersonally schizo. In the East they're kind of like, yeah, we're evil tyrants. Big deal. What goes around comes around. When you built a wall two centuries before Christ and it's still standing, I guess you tend to take the long view of things. We can't build a subdivision that doesn't collapse in thirty years. The evil Dr. B. is a scapegoat. We consolidate all our fears and anxiety about ourselves in his diabolical genius. That's why I have to catch his ass."

"And Dr. Bones created Information Sickness?"

"While developing a new, patented fat-free foodstuff. Unproven, but yes. Absolutely."

"And your task as the—what have you written here under 'Position?'"

"Epic quester."

"And your task as epic quester is to foil this malignant purveyor of human misery?"

"That's the standard plot."

"So, you're telling us the fate of mankind rests in your hands."

I waggled Spunky. "Me and the Spunkster. Pretty fucked up, ain't it?"

"Outside of Dr. Bones, any desire to hurt anyone?"

"Well, I could have slapped that duck silly."

"Not thinking of hurting yourself?"

"I don't know. Do we still only hurt the ones we love? You're the one with the shingle, you tell me. Is it better to suffer the slings and arrows of someone else's outrageous fortune? Does raging against the dying of the light include traffic signals? Maybe I have MPD, Multiple Perplexity Disorder. One minute I'm half in love with easeful death, the next I'm singing the body electronic. When the Everlasting fixed his canon against self-slaughter, you think He included the Western canon? Say, whom's that bell tolling for?"

Boy, did that first dose of Thorazine lay me out like a patient etherized upon a table. My tongue lolled, my eyeballs spun in my skull like slot machine lemons, I poured sweat and my eyelids drooped. My fingers trembled when I tried to lay them on Spunky's keyboard. Night swirled, or I swirled through it, until I didn't know what had become unglued, space-time or me. In the morning, I ran to the toilet and purged meals I'd eaten in previous lives until my intestines felt clean as a new straw. My complexion resembled a Xeroxed copy of health. My teeth had grown fur.

"Better?" they said.

#

Chapter Whatever

"Man, you look like a shell of your former self, whoever that was." My volleyball partner Deke stood in my dorm room doorway, posters for his stand up comedy show in hand. "You should come, dude. Get out, loosen up. Stop hitting the books so hard."

A voice that came out of my face said I'd try.

While I was brain dead from medication, the Committee for Student Body President that my golf-crazed advisor had assigned me to, cordially summoned me. Dragged by the heels into their campaign office, I felt rejuvenated by the effluvium of civic enterprise and cologne. Everyone sported tasselled loafers and blazers, even the women.

"Where have you been all semester?" presidential candidate Kiley asked. He had hair like a parted chocolate bar and a complexion so rosy I thought he'd been quarried out of red granite. His smile could have doubled as Broadway footlights. If he'd ever done a wrong thing in his life, word of it hadn't reached his face.

"I need a speech writer. Somebody to spin my negatives into positives, my positives into Holy Writ. My equivocating should sound like the Magna Carta by the time you're done tarting it up. I need creative thinking. I need slogans expressing what's wrong with this great interstate university in five words or less. I need promises that sound sincere but evaporate instantly in the student body's mind so I can't be held accountable. More than anything, I need—"

"Some of what Will's on," Spunk chirped.

"Are you on something? We can't have any drug scandals. This is a Christian Coalition party. Alcohol only."

I showed Kiley and his aides my Thorazine prescription bottle.

"It's an anti-psychotic," Spunk informed them. "Common side effects include drowsiness, bizarre dreams, euphoria, depression, and paranoia. Perfectly legal. Discrimination due to psychological distress is actionable and will result in a lawsuit."

"You mean our speech writer is a nut case?"

"But creative," Spunk assured them. "You should hear the shit he makes up."

I'm going to intrude here and confess that this was a dark time. Even Spunk assumed I'd cancelled my cable subscription to reality. Well, fine. By act three nobody was willing to write a letter of recommendation for Hamlet, either. This is the way it goes with epic questers. Jesus in the Garden of Olives, Han Solo thinking Luke had lost his mental light saber. Self-doubt creeps into every quest. All quests become tests of faith. I was determined to track Information Sickness to its source. And, as every quester learns, something may not be real, but that doesn't mean it isn't true. Everything is relative, including the truth.

Kiley sized me up. "I need somebody with a vivid imagination," he said to Spunk.

"Then Will's your drone."

Kiley leaned over and stared into my eyes, which felt like two 'For Sale' signs. "Quick, give me a campaign slogan."

"Kiley—Why Be Slowed By Scruples?"

"Let's say I support a university increase in student fees, but the hike includes frequent flyer miles and theme park passes. How do we sell my position?"

"Blending education with entertainment. All work and no play..."

"What if it leaks out that the Christian Coalition platform is funded by corporations polluting and enslaving the Third World?"

"Free beer for everyone."

"I'm caught in a sex scandal."

"We should all be so lucky."

Kiley leaned back. "Perfect. His idiotic cynicism is 100% in touch with our target audience." Kiley stood and began pacing. "For too long we've sought only to represent the self-righteous. Too long have we claimed that grade inflation lifts all boats. Too long overlooked any fellow student who wasn't fully invested in the market, or willing to genuflect at every photo opportunity. The apathetic deserve a voice that will feign interest in their lives, too. It's time to stop blaming everybody who disagrees with us, and accept them despite their flaws. Didn't Jesus say, 'Losers are people, too'? It's time to stop treating the despicable with contempt, and time to begin patronizing them. And, although we're superior to, and more deserving of wealth, privilege and power than anyone else we'd care to name, it is finally time to pretend that all men are brethren for the sake of political expediency."

I don't know if these were the words coming out of Kiley's mouth, or if the Thorazine was translating his thoughts into a kind of radio only the medicated could tune in to. When Kiley and his apostles DaVincied on me in a Last Supper pose at the headquarters buffet table, I began to suspect I might be experiencing side effects.

"I need a speech," Kiley said.

"I'm not feeling well. Plus, I believe university politics is a puppet show designed to bilk student fees to pay for keg parties and dry-cleaning your blazers."

"You're failing everything."

Either Spunk or I mentioned my pending A in "Hollywood and the Existential Tradition," if my quest generated a movie deal.

"We could implicate you in the Information Sickness plague," Kiley said.

Is it possible I actually said, "I have faith in the American judicial system"?

"I can have Naomi's Virology grade reassessed by computer to veterinary school acceptance range. Or, you can explain to the hottest piece of poontang this side of the Mall of America what an impotent lame-brain fuck up you are."

This was a neuron puzzler, all right. Naomi might never marry and love me until we wound up in counseling, then disclosed our intimate personal histories on the Divorce Channel, but at least she seemed to be flesh and blood. Crystal Goodlay might have been no more than a manifestation of my twisted libido. I'd been raised on lingerie catalogs, the Fashion Channel, pantyhose commercials, obligatory sex scenes and cheerleaders. Yes, cheerleaders. I don't care if Freud is discredited. When I see nubile flesh in a Danskin and panties twirl a baton across her vagina, what am I supposed to think? What precision! I'm nineteen. I get a boner if the anchor lady wears a new sweater.

At least, I did before prescription drugs turned my sex drive into a fond memory. Hoping it would return, I decided that nursing my fantasies about Naomi would be therapeutic.

"He'll do it," Spunk said. "He knows Realpolitik when he sees it. But don't think he subscribes to your anti-democratic impulses.

He comes from a long, noble line of failed revolutionaries. Before his incarceration, his father campaigned for McGovern. Mom burned her bra during her Homecoming Queen parade. His grandparents sold their votes to JFK's old man. Four NBA scores and thirty Super Bowls ago—"

"Say," Kiley asked the Spunkster, "how do *you* vote?"

"Big business all the way. If corporations had to pay a cent in taxes, I'd be a figment in some techno-nerd's imagination."

"Boy, I can't wait till elections are held online," Kiley crooned. "Meantime, I need a campaign button slogan, now." He looked at me.

I considered why anyone would want to be student body president and what effect a new executive would have on improving student lives, then said, "Kiley—Who Gives a Fuck."

Somehow, they read it in a positive light.

#

The Battle of the Sexes Rages On

Naomi, on the other hand, appeared far less inclined to read my actions in any form resembling sympathy. Her sitcom had gone into turnaround so she was back in school. She went ballistic when she found out I hadn't been doing her homework. "How am I ever going to get into veterinary school, you—!" her voice mail message profanely inquired. Meanwhile, I was happy I'd ordered call screening with my university telephone package.

Two days later Naomi turned up in the flesh, glowering at my Crystal Goodlay wall calendar when I opened my dorm room door. "You putz-puller. You hard-cooked my embryos!"

I suppose I had spaced harvesting the chicken embryos I'd set in the Virology Lab's candling machine while I was off questing.

If I *had* been off questing. People seemed to be doubting me. But, traditionally, disbelievers did not include the hero's beatific one true love. She with the hymen tight as the skin of a bongo.

"How am I going to keep my 4.0 GPA? I'm going to have to become some babyboomer's concubine to get into medical school. I hate you. You boiled baby animals. Everything was supposed to be perfect perfect perfect!"

Obviously, I wasn't the only one who needed an anti-psychotic.

"And *then*, you have to go have sex *online* with that…"

"Goddess?"

"She's had sex with rock stars! She's diseased!"

"Who told you it was online?"

Naomi pretended she had ethics by resorting to silence in order not to reveal her source. I glared at Spunk, who sat on my bed.

"Pretty interesting fact on the Web here, boss. Did you know that black men are 98% water? That's why there are no great black swimmers. Their skin's heavier, too, because of all that melanin."

"I should put you back in the box you came in."

How could I explain to a system that "believed" every fact floating in cyberspace was true that the foundation of all human relationships, particularly romantic ones, was lying. Love doesn't make the world go round, false promises do. What else creates false hope?

Naomi remained in ice queen mode. "Don't blame Spunk for your perversions. You'd hump a bean bag."

I knew it probably wouldn't stand up in court, but I said it anyway. "I can't help it if I was raped by a supermodel."

"*Another* sick male fantasy."

"What, do women have a list or something? I was climbing the corporate ladder. If that required kissing a little booty, I did it for us. Crystal meant nothing to me. She's a sexpot, plain and simple.

You think I noticed that her skin slithered over my tongue like cream? I was trying to bring an evil corporate monster to justice."

Naomi huffed and crossed her arms. "If you were in such a hurry, why didn't you premature ejaculate?"

"It would have blown my cover. I had to please her to gain access to the maniacal arch-villain's lair, and earn after-school money. I know I possess all the standard, unflattering male qualities—self-absorption, immaturity, a tendency to repeatedly piss you off without having a clue as to why—"

"The loyalty of a snake."

"But you told me *not* to go into date mode."

"And you believed me?" Naomi dropped her internationally renowned derriere on my bed, which meant I was supposed to sit beside her, put one arm around her shoulders, and convince her that she was beautiful, special and, as a specimen of human behavior, indistinguishable from the saints.

"Of course I believed you," I said. She pulled away, which meant, "Prove you want to hug me." I squeezed her Dallas Cowboys jersey harder. "I believed you because that's how much I love you—enough to set you free. Your happiness is all that matters to me. If you told me you loved me, but had to marry money instead, I'd be your bridesmaid."

Without looking at me, Naomi laid a hand on my leg.

"Of course, I want you to love me as deeply and eternally as I love you. But it has to be a free love, straight from the heart. Otherwise, what would we pass on to our children? A nice house, a big yard, two cars, and vacations every six months? I don't want them to get all their affection from our Golden Retriever, Becky. I *want* them to climb under the Ralph Lauren comforter to snuggle on winter mornings. I *want* to bore the shit out of people talking about them at cocktail parties. I *want* our daughter to walk down the aisle in white and, as I give her away to the world's leading neurosurgeon, have her say, 'Dad, thanks for risking your love for mom with that slut Crystal Goodlay so you could save mankind and give me the gift of marrying the man I've been living with while we worked out a pre-nuptial contract guaranteeing me 35% of his lifetime pre-tax earnings.' We'll call our grandchildren together long distance every Sunday, like we have nothing better to do with our lives. We'll take retired group cruises and read about adverse reactions in *The Pill Book* together. But more than anything, I want you to want me. You're my one true love, Na. Plus, I've sold my integrity to spawn of the religious right in order to get your A back. What do you say? Friends?"

Naomi turned to me, her eyes glassy as liquid gel caps. The sniffles were Spunk's.

"Oh, Will. Do you really love me, sitcom or no sitcom? And really, an A?"

"Yes. And I don't care about a stupid sitcom. Women love men for money. Men love women during their childbearing years for their bodies. I loved you even before I saw you airbrushed onto a haystack."

"I don't know who I am anymore. It used to be so simple. Daddy's girl, ballerina, musical comedy star, prom queen."

"You weren't class valedictorian?"

"No, the bastards gave it to some bitch with glasses. I'm sure she blew the principal."

"People are shallow, Na. They only see you as a fox and an airhead."

Naomi pointed her magenta (sic) eyes at mine. "What do you see, Will?"

The combination of Thorazine and Lithium had blurred my vision so I was seeing double, on top of strange colors. What was I going to tell her? *Both* your faces are gorgeous? "I see ... "

"Somebody ready to put out!"

I could see why Crystal had booted Spunk off the couch.

"I see...the woman I want breaking my balls for the rest of my married life."

Naomi melted, and I climbed aboard the puddle she made in the center of my bed. Our jeans slipped away like ripe fruit falling from a farming conglomerate's tree. Time stopped like a scoreboard clock as she took me in hand.

"What's wrong?" she whispered.

I assumed she was referring to my extraordinarily placid appendage. "What's the rush? A bird in the hand is worth two in the bush."

After an hour of Naomi yanking it like a vending machine handle with no success, I had Spunk boot up Thorazine's side effects.

"Bronchial spasms, loss of facial color," I read. And there, in microscopic print at the end of the two page list, "Impotence."

Naomi stroked my head and said she understood. "I think it's sweet. My high-school boyfriend used to shoot his wad before I could even get my hand around the thing. It was like dating a 'This Can't Be Yogurt' machine. Let's just cuddle."

Spunk lay under the covers with us, purring like a cat. A premonition of what marriage would be like shivered through me.

I thought an epic quester was supposed to receive a magic potion from the local shaman to make him potent and immortal, not a limp-dicked vegetable. I felt like an eggplant with arms.

Naomi and her famous behind fell asleep.

Fucking doctors.

#

In which I Once Again Seek Sage (And Now Sponsored and Copyrighted) Advice

Recollecting events in medicated tranquility did nothing to convince me that Information Sickness no longer imperiled mankind. In fact, I realized that people's obliviousness to the threat made the disease even more insidious. Obviously it had mutated, as viruses do, into a form detectable only by me. That people were willing to go along with the cover up meant the virus induced sheep-like behavior in the inhabitants of a once robust republic. Even the reports detailing the emergence and spread of Information Sickness I'd read in the student newspaper had been expunged.

"We pulp that rag in twenty-four hours," a testy librarian informed me. "Recycling preserves a tree? Save the planet? You know?"

I explained that recycling efforts were not cost-effective, and destined to go the way of the electric typewriter. "Pulp prices have dropped fifty percent. Only thirty percent of recycled paper ever *gets* recycled, twenty-five percent of bottles and cans. The rest is barge trash."

"Well, Mr. Smarty Pants, I guess you told me."

You see? People were afraid to know things.

The Center for Disease Control told me no information on Information Sickness existed. Decoded: Information Sickness is classified. For your contact lenses only.

I'd love to trust the institutions controlling my life, if only one would give me a reason to. God's silent; bureaucracy's sneaky.

Or maybe Thorazine was making me paranoid. I began to wonder what came first, my psychosis or my prescription. I'd swear I was less crazy before I was diagnosed, and billed, as insane.

For counseling, I turned to the "Socrates of Cyberspace," the "Freud of Fiber Optic Lines," that "Web Wizard" himself, according to promo material on his new homepage, the inimitable, and largely ineffable, Mr. Philosophy.

"Dear Wisest of All Mammals," I wrote.

"You probably don't remember me, if you're even the same, or the *real*, Mr. P. How do I know you're who you say you are? You could be some fireman killing shift time somewhere. With your popular Web site picking up corporate sponsors, how do I know your advice hasn't been tailored to send me subliminal messages to buy buy buy?"

"Hey, subliminal," Mr. P interrupted me, "try this for a secret message. Get to the fucking point."

Seems Mr. Philosophy had gotten crass in his attempt to build a media empire.

"Well, I may be having mental problems."

"How old are you?"

"Nineteen."

"Go get laid. Trojan condoms. If they're good enough for a horse, they're good enough for you."

"That's the thing. I can't get it up."

"You call this a *mental* problem? Kid, stick your head up your ass and have a talk with yourself."

Mr. Philosophy sure seemed different. I guess the Darwinian marketplace was getting to him. "No, you see, I can't get it up because of my medication."

"Well, maybe you're not taking *enough* medication. Did you ever think of that? Or are you waiting for a *subliminal message* from the pill bottle?"

"The side effects are making me paranoid. I think."

"You think? Hey, everybody, I *think* I'm Joseph Stalin! Don't you ever stop to consider that your narcissistic paranoia denigrates the people who *really* suffer? Here at Metro Life, we care. You can't say that about yourself, can you?"

"I'm trying to save mankind. I've been drugged because—"

"Of course. Because you're so close to the heart of the conspiracy. Like the car that runs on bubble gum the greedy oil companies have suppressed. And Exxon: Dedicated to Exxcellence.

Amoco: Aiming to please. When you go, go Conoco. You mean those conspiracies? Or the kind of conspiracy linked to nut?

Socratic dialogue evidently had sunk to a new low.

"So you're medicated, your dick is mushier than a six week old banana and, yet, you've discovered a top secret conspiracy. What do we have this time? UFOs carting off babies? Extraterrestrials in the White House? Satanic code broadcast as stock market prices?"

"A plague. Information Sickness."

"Ah, I see. And Information Sickness does what, exactly?"

"Spreads like a virus. If you know and understand too much, you begin to connect everything. When you see how everything's connected, but still makes no sense, you get ill."

"Maybe mentally ill?"

"Maybe. But heart disease, cancer, stroke, too. Information alters human physiology. Stress is caused by processing of information. Stress leads to strokes. Stress hormones trigger higher fibrinogen levels, thereby clotting blood cells and causing heart disease. Depression increases the risk of heart attacks four fold by increasing Cortisol production, which raises LDL cholesterol levels. Cancer has been linked to viral origins. So, information may actually be a type of cancer. Information Sickness could be the Tower of Babel in viral form. The Bubonic Plague spread by media."

"You hear that, folks? It's so obvious I'm surprised the rest of us missed it. Maybe it's because our heads are screwed on too tight."

"We have pictures of the edge of the universe."

"The Big Bang is a Kodak moment."

"We've found proof that an asteroid hit the earth 675 million years ago and killed the dinosaurs. We can do brain scans that show what synapses words originate in. We've created a synthetic membrane that allows human cells to grow around computer chips. Yet ... "

"*Yet* is history, thanks to Eli Lilly. Merck: Knitting the raveled sleeve of care. Pfizer: For postmodern living."

"At the center of all this information, don't you feel an emptiness?"

"Deconstructionists say there is no center, no moral objectivity, no truth."

"Isn't that a convenient philosophy for Nazi collaborators? Also, if there's no truth, how can what deconstructionists say be true? Don't you think postmodernism's attempt to flatten existential responsibility into a miasma of relativism actually performs an unwitting service for global capitalism? We know the Air Jordans we're wearing have been made by someone chained to a stitching machine in the Third World, but we buy the shoes anyway."

"And the shoe company's stock, if you're smart. Why fret? Just do it."

"That's the thing. Through information, we understand all the implications of our actions, but we act anyway. We're all compromised. Living in the 21st century means being morally and ethically numb."

"Look, you want existential solidarity, go play an old U2 album. I liked them when they started wearing sunglasses. People want to *dance*. I need grief about as much as I need a brain tumor."

"Benign brain tumors are quite common, and successfully removed by surgery, although they often grow back. Doctors are puzzled by the increase in brain tumors from 55,000 per annum in the 1980's, to over 100,000 today. 20% of these originate in the brain. 80% are cancers that spread to the brain from other areas of the body."

"*Why do you know this?*"

And then I realized something. *I'd* contracted Information Sickness!

"You want my advice? Go out, get blotto. Totally shit-faced. Up your medication. Take some plain Robitusson. Thins mucous secretions. Maybe you've got some sinus thing going on and it's fucking up your thinking."

"You don't think there's an evil capitalistic plague being spread by Dr. Bones?"

"First, why *kill* consumers? Who else is going to buy things? Second, Dr. Bones is a great humanitarian. Before he perfected no-fat meat and cheese, my pants seat was the size of a bed sheet. I ballooned if I even *thought* about a quarter pounder with cheese. Now I pork out with a clear conscience. Domino's deep-dish sausage pizza. Arby's bacon burgers. Chili's chicken wings with Roquefort dipping sauce."

"Barbecue?"

"I *love* barbecue," he growled. "I'd eat a baby if it was smoked right."

I recoiled in horror. I'd never recoiled before. I was usually like, yeah, whatever. But this revelation zinged through me like a visit to the electric chair. Mr. Philosophy's fat-free diet unmasked him as none other than the well-read doppelganger and perhaps corporate partner, of the evil Dr. you know who.

Western metaphysics—co-opted by the man who made fat-free food taste like polyester! The philosopher-king cloned from a CEO with an Elvis jones!

Boy, Plato's eternal form must be spinning somewhere like an Olympic discus.

#

In Which Everything Is Not Fun, Fun, Fun

Being psychotic, I quickly realized that Information Sickness and the death of metaphysics were linked, like a sitcom and its spin-off. My heroic duty was clear, despite the tremors and blurred vision from Thorazine and Lithium. Destiny had charged me not only with rescuing mankind from Information Sickness, I also had to resuscitate the corpse of the Western philosophical tradition if I was to win Naomi and once again be able to produce a noteworthy hard-on on demand.

So, I lay down and closed my eyes. Then I yawned. Then I was like, okay, here goes. I'm going to synopsize Western philosophy using Spunk's "Nutshellware" system. Man, was I tired.

Anyway, first: stopping to think made sense to Aristotle. With so little information in the ancient world, why not make a fetish of truth? What else was there to do, stitch a sandal? Imagining God or eternal verities killed an afternoon. It's what Hebrews did instead of renting videos.

We have the luxury of *not* having to think. We can flip channels, open a magazine, cruise the Net, clip on headphones.

Ancients were bounded in an imaginative nutshell, but considered themselves kings of infinite space. We have satellite TV.

After the invention of the printing press, people started getting metaphysically confused. Ideas were suddenly mass-produced. Socrates became just another opinion. The wise man yielded to the library, then to the newspaper and, ultimately, to the lowest of low, the columnist. Single, fixed, transcendent truth was retro.

The result: *adios,* objective reality! *hola*, subjective autonomy!

A century later, during the Renaissance, human imagination began to believe that it no longer simply copied images from divine originals made by God, but that it could create original images itself. Imagination elevated Man to the level of God.

But when Hume, an 18th century Mr. Philosophy and radical skeptic, thought about our new godliness awhile, he decided that if there is no transcendent truth, and all we know is ourselves through the human imagination, he'd rather play backgammon.

Then Kant cheered everybody up for about five minutes claiming that human imagination transcendentally synthesized worldly experience and our innate divinity. The Romantic poets were like, "Go, Manny!"

But being God got lonely for Romantic genius guys because everybody else was off building steam engines and factories and exploiting the poor. (There's always the poor. God, no God. Truth, no truth. The poor are always around to get fucked.)

So, finally, the Existentialists stepped in and said it was all a big joke. Men are gods? Just kidding, ha ha. Mr. Uber Philosopher himself, the Neitzsche-meister, told Western philosophy to get over itself. Transcendence is an illusion of the will to power. Truth is what we make up. Then ole Friedrich got the clap big-time and checked out thinking he had to save mankind. (Hm. Sound familiar?)

After that, the A-bomb kind of took the humanist fervor out of everyone, and most Mr. Philosophy guys bagged their act. Foucault claimed Man was "no more than a rift in the order of things," then donned leather chaps, got Greek in gay baths, and *au revoired* the truthless universe by not practicing safe sex and contracting AIDS. Derrida wrote postcards to dead white males, stating that every image is a mirror image looking at another mirror image, endlessly and forever, like being in an infinite television sales section at Sears.

So, with billions of equally weighted bits of information in the universe, what's any longer true?

The answer: nothing and everything. Eternal form becomes Windows XP.

End o' Western philosophy.

Big deal. Do you see me sweating metaphysical problems? No. Why? Because I'm a confident guy. Decision making for me is as easy as sort, share, duplicate, search. I've seen human indecision in action. Will putzes around for an hour before he can commit to using a semicolon. In, out, in. It's an independent clause for fuck's sake! This is not a bright kid we're dealing with here. You think *he* could synopsize Western philosophy in two pages? What's left of his brain is Velcroed to *TV Guide*.

Humans think they're clever. "Oh, look what we invented." Well, here's the dark secret: human ethics and behavior react to *us*, technological innovations.

The Industrial Revolution spawned Romanticism. Capitalism hastened the death of God. The Information Age will usher in the death of Man.

God died; the wheel's still (a)round. Think about it.

Waking up, I said, "Spunk, what's going on?"

"Oh, just playing a little chess here while you were napping, boss."

(And they say computers couldn't find a lap if they were sitting in it.)

#

In Which Everything Is Suspect

Refusing to be foiled in my quest by postmodern technology and psychiatry, I decided to go off my medication after rediagnosing myself as just Jim fucking Dandy. No laptop was going to synopsize Western philosophy while I napped, then lie about it—another stride for computerdumb, obviously!—as long as there was a single brain cell left in my head. I also didn't intend to have Naomi's internationally coveted butt naked and in bed with me while my John Henry lay there limper than a Tootsie Roll Junior in July. Within twenty-four hours of discontinuing medication, in fact, my manhood returned several times. I knew I was all the way back when my *Playboy* archive material finally arrived and I got a boner just looking at the bunny logo.

I guess I got a little manic too, because I cleaned my room, did my homework and worked out. I *never* work out. Muscles are fascism masquerading as flesh. I even outlined a campaign speech for Kiley to ensure an illegal, unethical grade change for Naomi through the Christian Coalition for Student Government.

Then I reported to work at the fog-shrouded hilltop laboratory, site of the pernicious, highly profitable experiments of Dr. Bones and, on this particular day anyway, a Crystal Goodlay photo shoot, which may have accounted for the lax security. I strolled past the guardhouse, glancing in to see Killer, the German Shepherd, looking mellow, his eyes glassy as melting ice cubes. Obviously Reefer, loitering up ahead near the photographer and his assistants, had imbibed with the pillbox door closed.

"Good Killer," I said. "Nice Killer."

On the photo set, Crystal wore what any Transylvanian *haus frau* would wear on a foggy day, silk panties and a bra that appeared to be made out of gold bullion. The photo captured her just as she happened to be sweeping the castle's drawbridge. Crystal didn't return my wave, even when I waggled Spunk over my head. Supermodels. One minute they come on sex-starved, the next they glare at you like you're a bounced check. The moral: don't expect loyalty from a babe in the Rent-My-Buns business.

"Man, I'd hold her dust pan any time," Reefer marveled as I came alongside him. We watched a make-up crew tint Crystal's haunches to cover blemishes, buff her already polished toenails and colorize her face with rouge. A personal assistant held a cigarette to the lingerie goddess' lips while Crystal dragged on it and, out of the corner of her mouth, screeched at her agent via cellular telephone. "This is the last time with these fucking outdoor shoots. You want your commission, get me a gig where I wear a parka! My ass feels like two pints of Ben and Jerry's."

Reefer offered to melt them.

One of the unadvertised features of cellular phones is that they can be easily thrown at people.

Reefer took cover behind the employee snacks vending machine that specialized in fat-free products licensed by the evil syntho-food maven himself, Dr. B. The array of choice was dizzying. For less than two dollars, I could take my pick of a warm cheese and bean burrito, a chili dog, fried potato skins, something called the Log of Beef, chocolate chip cookies and, somehow, campfire roasted marshmallows. If I turned around, I could watch one of the world's temporarily most beautiful women press her back against a fake castle wall like it was the most convenient place in the world to wear a camisole and look horny. Between the cheap food and the spectacle, it was kind of hard to stay motivated in my fight against capitalism.

"You know," Reefer said, weed diminishing his activist will, "sometimes being a prole ain't half horrible."

I recalled partying at Reefer's condo complex once. The sole redeeming feature of his apartment, besides his wide screen TV and a stereo deck as large as a refrigerator, was the fact that you could run straight out of the living room, leap off the second floor balcony, and land in the pool.

Inside the castle, I could feel the vibrations of successful profit hunting coming up through the soles of my shoes. Before me lay a roomful of the world's most beautiful, and mostly undressed women, each of them being fed experimental fat-free food products. I had infiltrated the evil conspiracy's operations center and I hadn't even punched a time clock.

"Fill the cup, leave it on the lavatory shelf," a voice said.

The personnel office stood directly beside me. I was offered a drug test container by the same Norse goddess who had led me into Crystal's lair. Perhaps it isn't fair to make comparisons, but after studying archival *Playboy* material I had to wonder if her breasts weren't something other than one hundred percent flesh. Historically, a woman's breasts, even after airbrushing, seemed to exhibit a modicum of sag, or flattening, depending on vertical or horizontal positions assumed by the body attached to said breasts. The pair I was staring at seemed to exist independent of gravity. I'm positive that if the woman walked away, her breasts were perfectly capable of hovering in front of me on their own like tiny extraterrestrial scout ships.

"Excuse me. But what are these made of?" I said, pointing impolitely.

"Screw the lid on when you're done. And don't forget to wash your hands."

My quest for scientific knowledge left her unimpressed. So did the noticeable bulge in my jeans when I unpocketed my hands to take the drug receptacle.

"Pig," she said.

At least my protuberances weren't cloned from radial tires. Or a fat substitute? Hm. The evil Doctor's mitts were copping capitalistic feels everywhere.

My quest for truth as an antidote to Information Sickness now forces me to narrate an unsavory scene that I believe is a first in memoir history. Memoirs depict incest, madness and domestic abuse freely. But lacking an epic dimension, none have confronted the drama of a central quester unable to urinate because he has a boner.

First, there is the problem of unsheathing Excalibur. Once free, it begins listing about, sweeping the area like a metal detector. At this point, any destination other than the ultimate Members Only club is bound to disappoint.

But while the drug testee may desire detumescence, the resilient organ has the force of nature supporting it. Depressing an aroused phallus is hardly as easy as throwing the switch on an electric chair in Texas. I had a stalagmite growing out of my groin. What if I pressed down too hard and it snapped off like an icicle?

Since this was an epic quest, I had time to seek legal counsel. I called Student Services on my cell phone but was informed that staff attorneys no longer handled underclassmen that were not incorporated. Noting the First Amendment issue at stake—what better example of free expression than a hard-on?—failed to elicit their patriotic fervor.

Spunky suggested I "Ask Al," after he completed a search for "Attorneys, Cheap."

The web site ad read, "Why pay to retain when I'm here to explain? Call 1-900-Pro-Bono and *Ask Al* about immigration, green cards, pain-in-the-ass landlords, creditors, disability claims and capital crimes." Al's credentials included an appearance on Court TV. I figured a guy who was such a big U2 fan that he picked a phone number saying he liked Bono couldn't be all bad. Even if he did charge three dollars per minute, like phone sex babes. Which reminds me. What's the difference between lawyers and prostitutes? After consorting with a prostitute you don't feel sleazy.

"Ask Al. For three a minute, I'm your pal."

"Hi. I'm on an epic quest."

"I don't do Supreme Court cases."

"First Amendment issues?"

"If they have commercial potential."

"I feel employer drug testing infringes on my Constitutional right to party."

"So, become an independent businessman. Free enterprise. You think I have to take a piss test?"

"But you're a privileged member of the ruling class."

"I work out of my fucking basement."

"Then you should be committed to ensuring the rights of the oppressed."

"Yeah? Why shouldn't I be more committed to ensuring the rights of oppressors who can pay. If I'm not paid, *I'm* oppressed. If I'm oppressed, how can I help you? Follow?"

I asked Al to consider that his rationalization merely disguised his exploitation of others for personal gain.

Exercising his right to free speech, Al posed a question that I declined to answer until I knew if we were talking airline flight, self-propulsion, mere alliteration, and who rolled the donut before I took a flying fuck.

Then I continued. "As a proponent of free expression, wouldn't you argue that the pursuit of life, liberty and happiness includes the right to an erection?"

"You're getting into privacy issues now. It's like shouting fire in a crowded theater. There's a time and a place for an erection. Phallic egress is not universally protected by the First Amendment right to assemble language."

"But I *am* in a private place."

"You're not in public?"

"I'm in an employee restroom."

"Single access, one at a time?"

"Except for the video monitor, I'm alone."

"Is your penis injured? We could have a Workman's Comp case?"

"My penis is fine. It's just too hard to point into the drug test container."

"How can you have a hard-on at work? I haven't had one since Watergate."

"I'm an epic quester and, as such, find myself in the evil arch villain's laboratory surrounded by an army of mostly unclad and excessively nubile babes."

"This always drove me nuts. Why would bombshells work as drones for fat ugly terrorists? They don't have boyfriends?"

"Two reasons. First, it's a sick male dominance fantasy, and untrue. Second, unoppressed late capitalist babes substitute materialism for maternalism. Until their body clocks begin to run down, they'd just as soon have a Ferrari as a baby. But, at thirty-five, babes begin to view babies as desirable consumer objects. Oppressed babes will never own a Ferrari, so they have babies at fifteen. Poverty limits oppressed babes to seven years of foxiness. Wealthy women can look sexy into their forties. Oppressed women increase their sense of self-worth by having children in a world that ignores and exploits them. Unoppressed babes increase their *net* worth, then worry about offspring."

"Where do you come up with this crap?"

"I have Information Sickness. It's kind of a trivialized omniscience. Like God being on 'Jeopardy.' I know everything but, you know, so what. The juxtaposition of omniscience and meaninglessness is making me insane. This is why I'm on a quest to foil the evil creator of Information Sickness."

"You don't need a lawyer, you need an exorcism. As for penile First Amendment rights, we run into *sentient being* resistance if we argue that an erection is a form of expression."

"But it is. It's a comment on my surroundings."

"So's a killing spree. You're bound by community standards for acceptable behavior. You're at work, you shouldn't have a boner, that would be the consensus."

"Not if I had a jury of my peers."

"So you're claiming that any—what?"

"Nineteen year-old hetero male not on Thorazine."

"—Would be *forced* into a state of arousal *against* his will? Hm.

We could initiate a sexual harassment case. These women are gorgeous and underdressed, right? We parade them to the witness stand. They huff at the camera as they answer cross exam questions about human sexuality. It would be like a pornographic Miss America contest. We'd be on TV for months. Look, don't worry about money. We pre-sell the trial rights. Headline: Boner Boy Sues Beautiful Babe Factory. Constant Erection Precludes Right To Free Choice! 'I'm permanently hard,' victim claims. You'll be a freak, but the culture absorbs these things. This is a burning human issue that demands to be brought to the public's attention. Stand up for—scratch that. *Crusade* for victims of priapism everywhere. Whine to the media. Get a book agent. Let me be your mouthpiece. We'll squeeze 'em till they ejaculate dollar bills."

His tone changed when he heard me moan.

"What ... why are you so quiet? You're pissing, aren't you?" Nothing encourages detumescence like legal conversation.

I placed the container on the shelf, washed my hands and stepped outside to punch the time clock, by which time my drug scan had been completed. As I only had antihistamines, enough decongestant to keep my heart racing ten weeks after I was dead, and traces of a major anti-psychotic in my system, I was cleared to join the post-industrial work force.

I had to hand it to Dr. B, he'd assembled a multicultural bevy of beauties in the name of corporate science. As I was led to my station, I passed Latino, Filipino, Afro, Euro, Indo, Sino and Anglo flesh, all of it cellulite free. It was like being at a human sashimi bar.

My work cubicle was a Plexiglas booth with bright lights. An array of experimental fat-free food served as my tools, everything from the lowly corn chip to *fettuccine quatro frommagi*. Amazingly, Dr. B had rendered heavy cream fatless. What next, a super-race of silicone women who would come WD-40? I'd gotten a boner over babes made out of something I sprayed on frozen door locks.

My cubicle partner appeared. For a moment, I thought I knew her. Then I thought I recognized her from a jeans ad. Finally I realized that she only looked like the jeans model because they shared similar faces, high cheekbones, sunken cheeks, and noses so chiseled they could be used as engraving dies. If she had breasts, they were flatter than housing starts during a recession. Her pallor resembled a raw oyster. The degrading test bikini Dr. B forced all subjects to wear made it clear this girl's diet began and ended with Tab.

My job proved remarkably simple, something even an idiot could do. And I thought, if Marx was right and workers should control production, would I feel any less alienated if controlling production meant I still spoon-fed diet test products to undernourished supermodel wannabes?

Gazing at the girl I had to feed, I couldn't help but think that if Eve had wanted to be a model, she wouldn't have reached for that apple. Perhaps Dr. B's misogynist corporate empire sought to avenge Eve, the first bulimic. She just *had* to have a snack. Now look where we are.

"Are you so thin," I asked, "because you mythopoetically reject any association with the image of a fecund first mother, since eating from the tree of knowledge now has us knowing so much that we die from it?"

She blew cigarette smoke in my face and I considered suing her for secondary smoke assault with malicious intent. "What am I eating today, fat-free walnuts?"

I ignored her rudeness and downloaded instructions from the mainframe computer. First task: take a body fat reading, tool provided. I lifted the fat detecting calipers and turned to her.

"I need to count what percentage of your body is useless pudge."

"No shit, Sherlock. Where'd they steal you from, MIT?"

"Maybe I should clip this to your brain."

I reached over and felt along her waist and hips for a place where my detector clips might find purchase. Her bare ribs curled like a melted radiator. I asked her to turn around.

"Don't you take vitamin supplements?" I asked, then latched onto a solitary ridge of fat squished into existence by the elastic band of her bikini. The meter registered 0.37%. Ten percent is the human norm. Professional athletes (excluding NFL lineman, who are notorious porkers) average five to seven percent.

"You're a fossil with a heartbeat," I told her. "How are you going to have children?"

She turned, scowling. "Americans are fat. Half the population over thirty wears stretch pants. Why do you think I'm overpaid to be here? I'm the ideal. Go ahead, feed me. I'll always look like this. You have to starve yourself."

I stuffed a croissant in her mouth. Her lack of nutrition had clearly colored her social prognostications. True, I'd realized that mankind teetered on the edge of grave peril. And, sure, maybe I had lost my mind. But you didn't see me sulking about the state of America. All right, maybe a little kvetching about capitalism. But mood is diet. If she chowed down on a Snickers she'd be singing the Pledge of Allegiance in no time. Dire cultural pronouncements are tough to make with a mouthful of cheesecake.

This got me thinking. If we are what we eat, then it follows that we're the hollow, bloated, physically and metaphysically undernourished nation of free marketers my skeletal supermodel partner suggested we were. Information Sickness could be the result of a diet of lies. Information without meaning is like sour cream without fat. We want to eat with abandon, so we create fake food. This is why information makes us sick. We gorge ourselves on it because we crave *more* when we should crave what's *true*.

I had it. Western philosophy could be revived if we stopped dieting!

"Are you all right?" my bikinied specimen asked. "You look like you ate a bad clam."

Actually, my metaphysical insight had made me nauseous. I swooned, then fell forward, my face smacking up against her growling stomach, thinking, girl you should eat something, as I passed out.

#

In Which I Reveal the Secret of My Melancholy

When I opened my eyes mom hovered over me like a detail of the Sistine Chapel in Website close-up. I was in my old bedroom at home, I think. The low, cottage cheese-textured ceiling, the pile carpeting that was standard issue in all subdivision units, the fake wood doors to my room and closet, it all looked familiar. It also looked like my dorm room, motel rooms I'd stayed in, all the rooms of all my friends and my mom's friends, and the rooms where Roger lived before he came to live with us. You can go home, just don't expect it to look different from the place you just left.

"Will, you're not making any sense," Mom said.

Which proves something else: everything is point of view. I think I've been making perfect sense. It was my mother that I was worried about.

So, I will shift narrative gears in order to reveal some intimate details about an episode mom and I never talk about, but which haunts me.

You see, before I was diagnosed and medicated, and long before I understood the necessity of my quest, my mother began to seem lonely, bereft. Perhaps a subtle strain of Information Sickness had infiltrated her system during one of her diet fervors. But, even before I came to understand Information Sickness, she had begun to seem inconsolably sad.

A few years ago A.D. (After Dad), before Roger turned up in her life, I came home from a high school kegger party where too many people had gobbled Rophynol tablets for a cheap buzz and turned into zombies. (One Roofie plus a pint of beer and the parking lot we partied in turned into the Magic Kingdom.) I expected Mom to be asleep. Instead, all the lights were out, a few candles were burning, and "Wild Horses" was playing on the stereo. I felt spooked, like I'd walked into someone's soul or something.

"Mom? You okay?" Most of her was in shadow, bits of her face and glints of her wine glass shining when caught by a flicker of candlelight.

She glanced up at me from the pullout couch that doubled as her bed. I slept in the bedroom down the hall. "Hm?"

"I said, are you okay?"

"Oh?... No." Then she laughed.

Drinking and listening to old music only makes you aware of how much of your life is gone. I knew this, and I was sixteen. It didn't help, either, that she was listening to a ballad about the end of childhood and lost love, alone.

Because she was my mother, I didn't think of her as either young or old, or with much of an interior life. She was sort of like the Ten Commandments, a big, imposing list of rules that loomed over me that I constantly broke. An obeyance machine, something programmed to civilize me without ever stopping to ask why or to what end. Thinking of her as human, someone with her own griefs and longings and, above all, beyond my power to save or protect, was just not something I did.

"You want to talk about it?" I said, sitting at one end of the couch. She just stared at me like—and I know it wasn't intentional or her fault or anything—but like I was a pale imitation of my father. Some joke version of him out of a movie where the husband/dad accidentally drinks experimental cocoa and morphs into, unfortunately, me. That stare told me how much I didn't know. That stare told me everything.

Then it melted and she recognized me again.

"There's nothing to talk about," she said. "Your mom is old, kiddo. I was your age a week and a half ago. Yesterday, there were all these great things I was going to do. Now, all the things I'll never do again, never *be able* to do again, outweigh all the things left that I can do."

I didn't tell her that she was being silly, that her life wasn't over, or that at forty-two she was still young enough to do whatever she chose. I simply asked her what she would never be able to do again.

"Kiss a boy. Have a boy tell me he loved me and not know what he was talking about. Stay out too late. Now, who gives a damn when I get home?" She swung her wine glass above her head, toasting her attachment to no one. "Have a baby," she said softly. Then, after a moment, "Kiss your father."

She stared down into her wine glass, rolling the liquid around in it as if sifting its residue for some wisdom to counter what she already knew. "I remember being at a party once with your father. He was talking or listening to somebody, I forget. Behind him was this young man. Although, I guess, then, I didn't think of him as young. We were all young. Only not so young that there weren't already things between your father and me, the kind of things you don't ... walk away from so easily."

"Like?"

"Like ... being crazy with grief together when our best friend died at eighteen, not in a car accident or from some rare disease referred to in eulogies as reminders of life's mysteries, but trying to save someone from drowning. Like being perfectly, blissfully happy with one another lying naked in bed, then losing that bliss when a first pregnancy you're both too young and broke and scared to handle comes along. Like...you.

"And in the midst of things not being perfect between your father and me appears this gorgeous young man. He didn't even realize how beautiful he was, I think he was too shy. He didn't know I was looking at him, either, which makes it easy to imagine people however you want them to be. We would never argue, I thought. Money would cease to exist, time would stop, just for us. Just to let everything between us be perfect.

"Then I looked at your father and ... I don't know... I couldn't imagine my life without him. It was like, here was this perfect lover waiting to be taken, and there was your father with all the mess we'd become. But I couldn't walk away from the mess because it would have been like walking away from myself. And what I wanted—what I *realized* I wanted—was two lives, the old one with your father and a new one with this gorgeous boy. And there was no way to have them both, fully. Which is when, and maybe this is stupid, I realized, I have only one life. This is it, I'm in it. And I'd never have that boy, never give myself to him, if I was to keep the other life I had with your father and me.

"Getting older just intensifies the feeling of how little we really get to be in the world. How small a taste of everything each of us, even the luckiest of us, ever comes by. Time makes us smaller by the second. And now I'm forty-two years worth of seconds smaller.

"So," she raised her wine glass and drank from it, "that's my Joycean epiphany for the evening. Or maybe it's a cheap red wine epiphany. I don't know, and I don't care."

"Why isn't one life enough?" I asked.

"Maybe it was, once. It's just with so much to choose from, with so many options, what's an ideal life? How do we know, when the only value is more? How can we live anymore and not feel cheated?"

After that night, maybe because she was alone, maybe because she sensed no resistance or judgment in me, maybe because she'd grown afraid, my mom talked to me about her longings and desires as if I were no longer her son. So, the first time she asked me to ride to the doctor with her I didn't think, okay, I get to skip school for a day. I knew we were going to see specialists and why we were going. My mother didn't want to think about why, even though all she did was think about why. So it became my place to do what she couldn't do.

We'd had an ice storm the night before we had to be at the hospital and the roads were deserted, power lines and trees glistening like the world had frozen and died. The medical center's heating unit had gone down. My mother and I sat in the cafeteria between her tests, huddled in our coats, sipping coffee.

"You sure you don't want cappuccino?" she said.

"I don't think hospitals should sell cappuccino." I'm not hungry, I told her when she ran down the list of things I could eat. Fruit, pastries, blackened fish, stroganoff, salad. "I'm fine. Why do you keep trying to buy me things?" She'd already offered me comics and paperbacks from the gift shop.

When the nurse called her name over the PA system, I walked her back to radiology. She took her x-rays from the desk clerk, listened to instructions as to where to carry the plain manila envelope next, then said thank you automatically.

When they summoned her into the specialist's waiting room, my mother asked me to hold her coat. She slipped the strap of her pocket book over one shoulder, smoothed her skirt and brushed back her hair, then kissed me on the forehead and walked further and further away until she disappeared behind a door leading to wherever she was directed next.

I know life flashes by. It flashes by because we live it in the past and in the future, always recalling what happened, or imagining what would happen next. Always next.

But to feel time's slowness, you need to sit in a cold gray hospital room with your mother's empty coat in your arms, when moment passes to moment, disconnected. To feel whatever was, or might be, freeze and break away from your life, like ice dropping off the limb of a tree. To surrender any illusion that you have any control over what comes … next.

Mom returned, her skin so pale it seemed translucent. "We have to wait to see someone else," she said.

"Who?"

"A surgeon." She said it quickly, as if that dissociated her from the situation, made it less real. I draped her coat around her shoulders and, after a moment, she put her hand on my leg. A moment later, I lay mine on top of hers.

The surgeon's nurse came out to get us long after the few people who had driven through the ice had come and vanished. The light outside the office window had gone from gray to blue-black, the deep blankness above the parking lot looking more bruised than asleep.

The surgeon came in carrying a Styrofoam cup of coffee. He wore scuffed white basketball high-tops with his hospital greens, the bags under his eyes spongy as poached eggs. Without introducing himself he said, "You have cancer. Some people like to dance around the issue and that's nice. But tumors are not nice, and while we dance, they spread." He looked at my mother, who looked like she'd just been hit with a bottle. "I'd like to go in tomorrow or the day after. Whatever's in there I want it out. The only tumor I trust is one that's in the bucket beside the operating table."

Mom sat there, shivering in her coat, and suddenly she looked smaller than I'd ever seen her look. She didn't glance at me. But she wasn't looking at the doctor, either. I don't think she was in the room, or even in the world, at that point.

My father should have been there, I know that. But the world isn't built this way any longer. People leave. There are so many ways to leave one another, so many other lives to lead. And maybe this was what my mom was thinking then, what am I doing in this life? I'm in the wrong room, having the wrong conversation. This is somebody else's life. This is somebody else's skin, someone else's disease. One moment, she was going to be here forever, the next she was gone, her life swallowed by the onrush of the world.

And so, as my mother couldn't speak, and my father was absent, I spoke in her place. "How do you know it's cancer?" I asked.

"From a medico-legal standpoint, I'm jeopardizing the patient and placing myself at malpractice risk if I don't cut to the chase. Cancer moves faster than e-mail. You want a second opinion on your golf swing, not on a neoplasm."

"But, you don't even know if it's malignant."

"Kid, what did you read, a chapter in your high school science book?"

Actually, anticipating this diagnosis, I had scoured the net, tapping into cancer research centers around the globe and downloading a volume of material as thick as a dictionary. "I'm not convinced it's even a tumor," I told him.

"Oh, okay! We'll just ignore the CAT scan and you can get your mother a crystal. Maybe that'll work. Or some herbal tea."

Then my mother snapped. "Why won't you listen to him?"

He threw his arms up like we'd announced this is a bank robbery. "Fine! I'm one big ear. Astonish me."

"Well, if it is a tumor," I asked, "why haven't we noticed any symptoms?"

"Sometimes these things are nearly undetectable until it's too late."

"Sometimes, not all the time."

"Yeah, sometimes," he said.

"So?"

"So."

"So, maybe this is one of those other times," I said.

"My job isn't to get your hopes up," he said.

"But you're overlooking the fact that she had pneumonia less than a month ago. What if the mass on the CAT scan is residual inflammation?"

"Well, we'll know once I'm inside, won't we?"

"But getting inside requires that you break a rib, no?"

"That's the entry price of a thoracotomy."

"And you compromise the lung by going in, right?"

He eyed my laptop, from which I read the questions I came prepared to ask. "You learned a lot of big words. What do they all mean?"

"That if a biopsy fails to produce a viable tissue sample, you can do a Video-Assisted Thoroscopy. The hospital has the equipment and you're listed as certified to perform the procedure. Right here." I turned my computer so he could read his name off its screen.

"I don't like VATs. They're time-consuming, and patients don't feel any less pain than a full blown thoracotomy."

"But the procedure doesn't break a rib or remove part of a lung."

He tapped his pen against my mother's chart and stared at me. Then he unsheathed the slides from radiology and popped them under the light board clips. When the fluorescents came on my mother's lungs spread across the wall like black waterfalls, a tumbling of webbed shadow and brightness. The disconcerting mass was a nearly round white spot the size of a walnut. The surgeon studied it, wishing, I'm sure, that the spot was a perfect circle, instead of attached to the outer edge of my mother's lung, which meant the image might—stress *might*—be pneumonia. He stood there a while longer, not looking at us, then said, "Fine. Suit yourselves."

The night before her operation, my mother and I took a motel room near the hospital. We ate in a strip mall restaurant that served fajitas, egg rolls and lasagna beneath giant TV screens. Back in the room, we stayed up watching movies we'd seen in theaters six months earlier. I drifted off at some point and when I opened my eyes during the night my mother was standing at the window, her white T-shirt bright from the access road lights and all-night eatery and motel signs. Maybe I asked her what she was looking at, maybe I didn't. I can't be sure. All I know is, she didn't hear me. At least, she didn't answer, as if she were already gone.

When we arrived at dawn, sleep-drained technicians, nurses and surgeons drifted through the hospital halls. Forms had been prepared for my mother and she signed them, asking questions I sensed she knew didn't matter. She had placed herself in the care of charts and machines, procedures and shifts. She was passed from the admissions desk to pre-op where someone drew her blood. Someone else took her blood pressure and, finally, someone asked her to remove her clothes and wrap herself in a gown worn and laundered so many times it had nearly disintegrated and was ready for the trash. Walking beside the gurney, I held her hand, the nurse telling her she had a handsome son, my mother squeezing my hand harder. Then the doors opened and I couldn't go any further and her hand slipped from mine, and all I could do was stand there.

After a while, I walked out behind the hospital. The sun had come up over new subdivision construction and the interstate. The cars in the physician's parking lot gleamed and, in the distance, cars filled the lots of computer and microchip plants so that they looked like steel flower beds. The mall hadn't opened yet, its green space a sheet of ice and deserted except for a few figures in white uniforms pushing snow blowers around its dormant trees and empty fountains. Back inside, I tried to read but the words bounced between the sounds of the waiting room television, pages for doctors, and ringing telephones, sticking to the signals around me rather than to the inside of my head. I wandered through corridors that led to corridors that looked like where I'd just been. In the gift shop, newspaper headlines screamed and magazine covers took me from place to face until I felt I'd come unstuck from where I was.

Time came and kept coming, all of it empty. As I sat in the waiting room again, I understood that we don't lose the past but the future. It's the future that comes and comes, hoping for us to fill it with life.

"Well, all I'm finding is inflammation," the surgeon said, taking a seat beside me. He tapped his fingertips against one another and looked at the floor, then glanced briefly at the television news and bits of the world floating by on it.

"Inflammation is good," I said.

"Inflammation is inflammation. I ran a frozen section and that's all it tells me there is. I'm not imaging a tumor on the VATs monitor, and I can't feel anything if I slip my finger inside the lung. But that doesn't mean there isn't a tumor, or that there won't be a tumor three months from now. If I stop now, there are no guarantees. Follow?"

I nodded.

"I can go all the way to be sure," he said. "It's your call."

"Stop," is all I had wanted to say, and all I said.

While my mother was in recovery, I crossed the access road. In the gourmet food shop next to the video/book store, I bought a plastic bottle of what claimed to be fresh squeezed orange juice and, past the bagel chips and imported African coffees and rows of all natural packaged foods, found an out-of-season rose wrapped in cellophane. Ice crunched underfoot as I made my way back to the hospital, and when my mother opened her eyes I handed her the flower that she took and held and, finally, pressed to her lips. And, even though both of us knew it smelled nothing like a rose, and that my empty orange juice bottle was a poor substitute for a vase, we made a home for it anyway, a place to blossom and, when the time came, die.

And what that gesture said to me was, meaning is neither permanent nor absolute. From moment to moment, what we think we know shifts and changes, for one simple reason—we're alive. Dying is only what comes. Dying requires only waiting. Living demands faith.

And maybe this is why I went insane, or seemed insane, for a while. Maybe I lacked sufficient faith for living. Maybe Information Sickness had wrenched all the faith out of me. Or, maybe I'm lying, making everything up. Inventing a story for a world that either resists meaning, or encourages so many multiple meanings that meaning itself vanishes and we lose our sense of who we might be, and what we might become.

All I'll say is, once I'd seen my mother surrounded by seas of information, yet at a loss as to why she had lived and why she should die, I began to see the world differently. I began to feel that questing is all. And that the quester neither succeeds nor fails, but lives moment by moment, if necessary beyond the rational, which is only a part of life. A quester does not wait, or let come what would come, but seeks—knowing there are no fixed answers, only hope; no end, only flux and rebirth; and beyond irony and despair, laughter, in which meaning and identity are reborn.

"Heavy," Spunk said. "I'm awed by the mysteries and narcissism of human existence."

See? This is what I'm talking about.

#

In Which I Rebound From A Long Flashback and Once Again Reap the Benefits of Modern Medicine

Perhaps I shouldn't have gone off my medications. This was the opinion of the psychopharmacologist(s) my mother took me to see again, following the laboratory episode. "We thought the Lithium was doing a pretty good job of keeping a lid on the manic hallucinations with little risk of blood toxicity," they told me.

"I couldn't get an erection."

"That was the Thorazine and, before that, the Haldol."

"I felt like an emotional dial tone. 'Your head's on fire!' 'Oh, bad?' 'God just reappeared.' 'Good, tell Him I said hi.'"

"Want to talk about your seizure?"

"You mean, when I blacked out in Dr. B's fat-testing lab?"

"Are you sure you weren't at your usual work table in Virology Lab?"

"Naomi would have been there."

"And she wasn't."

"No. I was spoon-feeding a beautiful, but emaciated, supermodel-in-waiting. Then I had a revelation. An insight into the contemporary information-laden world so powerful that it—"

"Brought on a seizure."

"No, I just understood things."

"Suddenly everything made sense?"

"Yeah."

"And you felt as if you had all the answers to the puzzle of existence."

"Sort of."

"Only?... "

"Only ... I didn't have the language to express them."

"But?... "

"But, for a moment, I felt like ... "

"God."

I thought about this. I tried to recall how I felt right before I fainted. The sensation seemed to mimic what I imagined being omnipotent and eternal entailed. Not that I felt bodiless. I just felt my body wouldn't ever age or die, and that all the mysteries of existence were known to me. But I also knew I couldn't communicate what I knew to others. I couldn't bring meaning into the world.

So I answered, "No, not like God. Like a demon. To know everything, but not be able to create meaning out of it is demonic, isn't it? God needed meaning. Otherwise, why create the universe? Why not just hang? Having all the information doesn't add up to meaning. Free will creates meaning. If everything's perfect, there *is* no meaning. Imagine the conversations in Eden. How was your day? Divine. And yours? You don't get meaning until Eve bites the big one. For meaning you need suffering and death and beauty and renewal. Pills or no pills, mankind was born to fuck up. And no prescription pad is ever going to change that." I may have even added, "So there."

They had to get the new pill down my throat with a slingshot.

"I guess this means I'm rediagnosed," I said.

#

Thou Shall Not Have False Dads Before Thee

I had the Spunkster search the online Physicians Desk Reference for a clue as to what new side effects I might be expecting.

It appeared that I'd been prescribed medication used to treat epileptic seizures.

"I thought you were bi-polar," Spunk said. "With seizures you're getting into Dostoevski territory. Religious visions, the Second Coming, conversations about God that go on for 150 pages but nobody even stops to go the bathroom. What are you taking, an anti-convulsant?"

"I guess." I was too defeated to check, which is why God gave me Spunk.

He read off a list of them. "Dilantin Kapseals?"

"That sounds about right. What are the side effects?"

"Hm. Well, I'd get ready for your brain to feel like it's experiencing a power failure. You're going to have less voltage running through the old circuits. Cuts down on the chances of seizures. You'll need frequent blood tests to make sure the drug isn't screwing up your red and white cell counts. Um, also your basic nausea, headache, dizziness."

"Got those already."

"Hey, here's a new one. Rapid or unusual gum growth."

I peeled my lips away from my teeth and examined my gums in my bedroom mirror. I realized that if my gums got so big they swallowed my teeth, I'd have a mouth like a vagina with the world's largest clitoris. "Impotence?" I asked, expecting the usual.

"Actually, I'm not finding any indications of that. Why? Important?"

I couldn't believe my luck. A medication that would leave me brain dead but penilely active. Just like Frankenstein.

But, as if reading my thoughts, Spunk said, "This is a weird one, though. Peyronie's disease. A condition where the penis is permanently deformed or misshapen."

What happened to quests where the hero was handsome? Now I was going to have a penis shaped like a bow tie.

"You look like you lost your best friend," Roger said when he came home from work. He set down his briefcase and took off his blazer. Then he cracked open a beer and popped a buffered aspirin like he did every day to reduce his chances of having a heart attack according to today's theories about heart attacks, which were bound to change tomorrow. "Anything I can do?"

I sympathized with Roger's position. As a stepdad with an average job and no particular awe-inspiring talents, he sensed that his chances for legitimacy in my eyes were nil. He would always be the impostor that had usurped my vanished father. Some guys may have responded to the situation with force or hostility, substituting meanness for credibility. Roger never did. He was content to let me seek his advice or not. And when I screwed up he let my mother handle things. But he did it all without ever making me feel I was beneath contempt because I was some other man's son.

So I said, "Yeah, you can do something. Answer a potentially dumb question."

"Shoot."

"Do you have faith in anything?" I knew he had faith in the erotic possibilities of Crystal Goodlay's homepage because he caught me having sex there. But that was one of those things neither of us ever mentioned, like masturbation, which we pretended was something that happened to other people. "Or do you think life's just one thing after another, and whatever happens is random and simply a matter of luck?"

"Oh, give him a break," Spunk shouted. "He just got home from work!"

Roger cleared his throat. "I think I'm a little out of my depth in that area, Will."

My mother came in the door after a day of typing contracts for a new action movie starring Goldilocks and the Three Bears as crime fighters.

"Will asked your live-in boyfriend the meaning of existence!" Spunk blurted.

Mom, knower of all things feminine and wise, decided it was time I got out of the house, epilepsy, bow-tied penis and all. For she was smart enough to know that nothing cures a case of existential despair faster than a dose of popular culture.

#

Containing Blues, Stand Up, Secondary Smoke, and a Revelation of Paradoxical Importance

After scanning the local "What's Doing" section of the paper and finding only tours by the World Wrestling Federation, a religious group holding a "Confess-O-Rama," an author signing copies of his latest best seller "LIFE IS GOOD, *PEOPLE* ARE BAD," and a junior high school production of "King Lear," my mother checked my backpack and found the flyer for Deke's comedy show. She dangled her car keys an inch from my eyes. "Go have fun. The meaning of existence can wait."

I suppose my driving was a tad rusty, because an inordinately large percentage of other travelers offered me the finger. I understood their frustration. Information arrived instantly; we still had to "yield." At least, in theory we did. Most of the drivers around me seemed to consider red lights "suggestions."

Naomi was waiting for me outside the girl's dorm.

"I'm kind of embarrassed that my mother called you to go out with me," I told her when she got in the car.

"Don't be silly. It was totally touching. Most moms think of me as a shotgun wedding waiting to happen. Hey, Spunk!"

"What ya say, Na?"

Naomi slid the tip of one finger sweetly and softly along my face. "How are you feeling?" she asked.

Suddenly I wanted all seventeen million copies and the original hayloft photo of her in my hands so I could burn them, thereby erasing every erotic connection of Naomi to anyone in the world but me. I didn't mention this to her, though, because I didn't want to have an argument about women as property. She could own *me* if she wanted to. All I wanted was Naomi's hand caressing my face for eternity. This was one of life's affirming moments. An instant when time stops and the world briefly feels untainted and reborn. I never wanted it to end. Sue me.

"I feel all right actually, as long as my penis doesn't curl up like a pretzel."

"It's probably just stress. Who can relax anymore? Even relaxing means deciding where to shop, what video to rent, what pizza topping to order. It's like, let me turn my brain off for half a second, please."

At the club, I pulled my mom's Plymouth "Steed" into a space beside a dumpster. A line had formed outside the club's door as most students were still reluctant to ingest potentially harmful knowledge by studying. Plus it was Wednesday, the perfect night to begin warming up for weekend partying, which began Thursday, so you didn't hurt yourself. Naomi was recognized instantly by a dateless contingent of males, one of whom said, "Hey, almost didn't recognize you with your clothes on."

"You couldn't recognize your hat if it was on your head!" Spunk shouted.

"Tell 'em Spunk," Naomi said.

"Pretty aggressive software," someone mumbled.

I shrugged apologetically. "Monkey see, monkey du-plicate."

Inside, Naomi and I grabbed a table near the small stage and ordered.

"Are the french fries real potatoes?" Na asked. Amazingly, they weren't a corn syrup product. "Good, I'll have the hand-cut fries, *lots* of melted cheese and a Guinness. He'll have the same." Then she handed the waitperson the menus and looked at me. "You need to fatten and cheer up."

"I don't know if I should drink while I'm taking major medication."

"I'm an almost veterinarian—please, God! In six to ten years, I'll be drugging hogs." She put her hand on mine. "Let me worry about it."

Then I had one of those revelations epic questers are prone to. "My mother told you I have a brain tumor. That's why you went out with me. This is a pity date."

Naomi tisked and sighed. "I'm going out with you, silly, because you let me find my way to you. You waited till I was ready and that's … romantic. Plus, you make me laugh."

"What if I stop being funny? You know, because of my brain tumor or Information Sickness."

Naomi tongued a just-arrived french fry into her beautiful mouth, looked at me irresistibly and said, "Then you'd better make a lot of money."

As the lights dimmed, Naomi ordered another pint of stout and a veggie burger with ranch dressing, and why I loved her became perfectly clear. Not for her coveted behind, which time would cause to spread, sag, ultimately wither and waste away. Her mortal coil had ceased to obsess me the moment I became impotent and turned my thoughts to a sentimental appreciation of the human spirit. No, I loved Na for her goodness, her desire for the truth, and for not dieting like the infernal spawn of Dr. B. I probably would have had tears in my eyes if I could have seen Naomi licking the fat from her fingertips through the club's haze. Instead I was like, buy a smoke eater!

A guy appeared on stage, carrying a guitar. "I'm just gonna play a bit while Deke warms up." He arpeggioed C, F, and G chords, which told me he'd probably launched his musical career about an hour and a half ago. "Growing up, the blues masters of the Mississippi delta were a huge influence on me," he explained, sensing the audience would make the connection between growing up in a white subdivision and slavery. "So this 12 bar blues is an homage to their artistry. It's called, 'Ramblin' Blues.'"

> Well, I was born to ramble
> But down which interstates I couldn't decide
> Said I'm genetically inclined to ramble
> But just past which strip malls I just couldn't decide
> Lord if I had me some brains I'd live in the woods
> Take some big ol' she-bear for my bride.
>
> Well, I'm an Information Age baby
> Know it all, but feel blank inside
> Said I'm a hi-speed, age o' info-mation baby
> Take news of global tragedy in stride
> And when that deservedly famous grim reaper
> Come to get me,
> I'll beat him (or maybe her) to it with assisted suicide.
>
> Said I was *in vitroed* to ramble
> And slouch on Naugahyde,
> Well the good Lord knows I'm neurochemically
>   predisposed to ramble
> I carry Amex and Visa by my side
> And when I get too old and crabby to ramble
> I'll call some big ol' travel agency
> And let the service industry be my guide.

"Man, talk about suck," Spunk complained once the guy had de-staged. "You can have the blues. Give me techno-hop any day."

Then Deke sheepishly took the stage, a narrow shaft of light from above barely illuminating him, his voice leaking out of near total darkness:

"I'll tell you, it's tough being postmodern.

"I walked into a video store. They had movies separated by budget. I rented something made for over two hundred million. The special effects included my television blowing up.

"I went to a bookstore and asked for something inspirational. They told me to look behind the Armageddon section.

"Is it me? What are the rules? What makes sense?

"I was watching a ballgame and saw a part of my fractured self sitting in the stands.

"The deconstructionist waitress at the coffee house told me there was no center when I tried to order donut holes.

"The Second Coming is the sign of a good date.

"If truth is beauty and beauty truth, why aren't supermodels philosopher kings?

"I heard about a baby born marked, 'Return Postage Guaranteed.'

"I went to a vegetarian restaurant run by Buddhists. The menu was in koans.

"I swear, I heard the sound of one hand clapping on a laugh track.

"I thought genetic engineering might help. They gave me a choice of moods—mellow, content, happy, exuberant. I went with mellow. My girlfriend left me for a Cub Scout. I was, like, 'Bye.' My boss fired me for lack of enthusiasm. I said, 'That's cool.' Somebody ran over my dog, Commander Burnside. I thought, whoops. Then I wondered if I missed having feelings, so I went for testosterone injections. When the cashier asked if I was paying by cash or check, I head-butted her.

"Is asking what the point of existence is the wrong question?

"I got a telemarketing call for nuclear weapons.

"I went to church with a friend. The donation box took Visa. I went to communion. Before I took the host, the priest said, 'Whole wheat or white?'

"If all is vanity, there won't be any meek to inherit the earth.

"Is there just too much of everything?

"Is information the end of meaning? You tell me.

"Because I don't have a clue."

Then the spotlight expired and Deke vanished. I wondered if he and I could become the first metaphysical action heroes. Instead of using high tech weaponry, we'd subdue evil with aphorisms.

But riding home in the afterglow of the evening's entertainment, evil suddenly seemed to me as much a part of life as beauty. The fat-free virus Dr. B. had created would continue to replicate. The plague would spread. People would live and people would die. Why? Because the real plague was life. And as Naomi and I rolled along the interstate, I realized two things: that my powerlessness to change life was part of my quest too, and that my faithful Steed had cruise control.

Wow! If this were a novel, I'd be screwed. My epic epiphany was an anti-epiphany. But, what can you expect when the illusion of a hero conquering evil and restoring order to the world is handled by Prozac?

Fortunately, this is an epic memoir, not fiction, so my quest continued, regardless of consequence or import. And for days all I could do was crack the mailbox, wait for the life changing phone call that would never come, and hope that maybe something interesting would happen.

Geez! No wonder writers make shit up.

Containing Words, Words, Words

Then, Kiley called from his campaign headquarters.

"I didn't bribe you with a grade change so that you could go inhale secondary smoke at liberal comedy clubs. I need verbiage. Have a speech for me today or die."

Thus, I found myself thrust back into the grand pageant of civilization. Kiley's political platform was refreshingly simple. He'd left out the usual hollow rhetoric about progress and change, about equal representation for all, and cut straight to the heart of the matter. "I wanna be President!" My job as Kiley's speech writer was to create the illusion that his egomania might be entertaining enough to hold the attention of the student body throughout the grueling two day campaign.

"Spunk, it's time to get to work," I said, "lest Na lose her A, and me her precious boo-ty." Obviously, my new medication had slowed the electrical impulses in my brain by about four centuries. If I regressed any further, I'd be speaking like Beowulf. However, political speech writing, I discovered, did not require a fully active brain. So, after some false starts, some sitcom breaks, lunch, and a nap, I made swift headway, milking contemporary culture's wisdom for the best that had been thought and said in the last five minutes. I arrived, speech saved on disk, moments before Kiley's appearance on campus cable access TV.

"How do I know this is any good?" he shouted as underlings beat me about the head, which definitely didn't do my brain tumor any good. That is, if my psychopharmacologist(s) weren't once again wildly guessing and magnificently, but billably wrong about me even having a brain tumor.

"The culture's beyond good or bad," I told him. "There's only next."

"I haven't had time to rehearse."

"You'll seem spontaneous."

"Voters distrust spontaneity."

"So? Voters don't win elections, money does."

Kiley hesitated, wondering if anything he said to the cameras might actually matter. Then, with the grim resolve of a born leader said, "Finish my makeup," and took his place in front of the vast, uncaring video audience, with Spunk as his teleprompter.

"My fellow students. Why pretend any longer that, when elected, I either hope or plan to accomplish anything beyond enriching myself at your expense? Greed and the delusion that I'm wonderful are my sole motivators. And I, for one, say it's high time that politicians stop clinging to sentimental rhetoric and admit their venal ambitions. Gone are the days of the sports hero. Vanished are the times when movie stars hid their contempt for the audience. *Au revoired* the CEO's false shows of concern for employees. Why, then, hold politicians to obsolete standards of pap?

"I have a theory.

"Because we are so useless, so disposable, so craven in our lack of purpose, that we feel obligated to humiliate ourselves by lying outrageously in public about what we hope to accomplish. This is a disgrace. But, disgrace is a politician's only entertainment value. If I could hit a jump shot at the buzzer, you'd better believe I'd be telling you all to kiss my ass. And if I grossed $100 mil in domestic box office every time out, I'd be bottling my piss as after-shave, too.

"But I'm a different class of anti-humanist scum. I prey upon hope. I ask you to examine the part in my hair and imagine a brighter future. I'm a spectacle of dishonesty and ineptitude. So what. I'm going to win the election anyway. Do you think I'm going to do anything about escalating tuition? About being instructed by teaching assistants who are two weeks out of high school so professors can give papers on 'The Caesura in Contem-porary Canadian Prose Poetry'? About soft drink conglomerates endowing Distinguished Chairs in 'The History of the Jingle'? I'm elected by these people, whose business is to exploit you. And your task, as students, is to learn just enough so that you'll be able to exploit people when *you* graduate.

"There is no capitalist conspiracy. *We* are the conspiracy. *We* buy the software and the soft drinks. *We* don't care if a megalomaniacal dunderhead like me gets elected. *We* are the truest of true democracies. *We* have got the leaders and the shabby culture we deserve. And the world is welcome to share in the bounty of dreck we produce—for a price. For this is the meaning of America: to stand for nothing, and charge for everything. Some say we lost our moral compass when we stopped owning people. Others say that empires are built on the backs of slaves. But I say *we* are moving toward a cultural, political, and economic slavery to the marketplace that will once again make us great. And, when the market fails, *we'll* become religious fanatics!

"Being American means to energetically pursue an empty future. Being American means possessing the freedom to have conversion experiences based on something you read in a magazine article. Being American means having the liberty to be a bundle of paradoxes. And being American means you can rest assured that the hour of our greatest glory and our deepest shame are only five minutes apart.

"I cannot lead you because you will not be led. Who better, then, to govern your affairs than someone without vision? The Campus-Under-the-Fighter-Jets-Flight-Path stands squarely in the American tradition of pursuing profit under the guise of lofty purpose. Of letting the moment at hand define who we are. And, as we slalom onward, I promise, when elected, to stand idly by and do nothing, except maybe play golf.

"Don't vote your conscience, vote your pocketbook. A vote for Kiley is a favor unreturned. God's silence means you should speak up. No taxation without representation applies only to Fortune 500 companies. If you're not happy, wait five minutes. Give me liberty or give me wealth. Honesty is the best policy if you've done nothing wrong.

"So join me while I chant:

> Order that pizza
> Watch that show
> Illegal campaign contributions for Kiley
> Are the way to go!

> Peddle some influence
> Spread that cash
> Expose corruption in the papers
> Then throw 'em in the trash!

"Let's sing!

> Well, I'm venal and I'm sleazy
> Not an idea in my head
> If you think moral bankruptcy is easy
> You're un-American and a Red

> Yeah, I'm shameless and I'm greedy
> I check my scruples at the door
> I starve the arts and tax the needy
> When I'm down I go to war!

My tax code is infernal
And I'm such a fucking boor
But I'm vile and eternal
so there's no use getting sore

You'd need a magician or mortician
To make room for another whore …
Who'll just lip sync my position
And screw you to death's door!"

Kiley was still strangling me when the polling booths closed and the vote was tallied.

"It's a landslide!" he crowed. "I captured 66% of the vote! I have my mandate!" He'd crushed his opponent, two votes to one.

"What boob voted for Kiley besides himself?" I mused. Spunk remained disturbingly silent. "You didn't."

"What? He's not so bad. What's wrong with software companies designing curriculums anyway?"

And so, just when it seemed that my life had plummeted to the anti-zenith of meaning, Naomi was kidnapped by the evil Dr. B.

My epic quest once again cried out for consummation! Out of the tedium of ordinary days is born the test of heroes.

Who'd a thunk it?

#

In Which I Break Point of View (Again) and Discover the Meaning of Existence

Meanwhile, back at Old Man Cotter's ramshackle bait shop, word of evil's latest machinations was being hotly debated.

"Seen in the paper where that Crystal Goodlay's marrying some prince guy?" O.M.C. asks, touching up his dentures with white out, while listening to his new passion, National Public Radio.

Sheriff Bill looks up from the twelve-inch color TV Gus keeps tuned now to PBS and ruminates, "She always seemed like a nice girl. Wholesome. Kind of the girl next door type you'd like to come home and find in a teddy and Air Pennies. Don't see what she ever seen in that evil tycoon Bones anyway."

"What you suppose changed her mind? Maybe he slipped her some a that Information Sickness."

"Gus, there ain't no such thing as Information Sickness. I work over to the college. Do I got Info-mation Sickness? Do I know everything? Infer-mation Sickness is some fantasy cooked up by lamebrains don't know how to be happy. They want one answer to the myriad questions and dilemmas postmodern industrial life poses, and there ain't one. We got micro-problems, not one big macro-problem. It's just people got fixated on the Bomb. And now that they've gone and forgot about it, their brains is still in One Big Problem mode, which made life kinda easy to figure. The feller with the Russkie Bomb was evil, everybody else was either good or afraid we'd kick their ass. Information Sickness just wants to replace the Bomb. Well, can't be done. Meaning's scattered like a blast a buckshot. Mostly always has been. Heck, G.C., after all, we ain't but crawled out of the sea a million years ago. The universe is twenty-three billion years old. We're young-uns. We got time. We'll figure it out."

"Now you upped and went Darwinian on me?"

"Shoot, did I?"

"Next you're gonna be telling me Genesis was a dramatization. Or worse, made up by some patriarchal scriptwriter got dumped by his girlfriend so he blamed the Fall on a babe. Which is why women like Crystal Goodlay feel psychologically compelled to get trussed up like rodeo animals. All those straps make a man feel like he's in charge. It's an erotics of domination. No wonder she's marrying a prince. He won't jump her bones for ten minutes every three days. Princes want wives for in public. They get sex-a-plenty with the royal concubines.

"Gus?"

"Festus?"

"How'd we get so g.d. brainy all of a sudden?"

 Gus's eyes narrow stereotypically and his forehead glows like a steamed lobster. "Man, I hate being an expendable minor character. Butch and Sundance homoerotically bonded through a pretty schoolmarm, then went out in a hail of bullets. We fade into oblivion listening to NPR. And all because you hadda try that new fat-free gravy. You couldn't just eat eleven portions of fruit and vegetables a day, which studies show are just as effective as beta blockers for lowering blood pressure and reducing LDL cholesterol levels."

"Gus, since we got smarter, you feel any different?"

"I'm kinda over everything, if that's what you mean?"

"Any clue as to the meaning or purpose of existence?"

"Not a one."

"You figure maybe the answer is one a them Kierkegaardian leaps of faith? You know, shake the despair that comes with the realization that human understanding and eternal truth are about as compatible as a fish and a bell jar. Old Sören warned us reason weren't gonna do us no good."

"Now don't we have enough fundamentalists going around with a snapshot a Jesus on their dashboard without you jumping in? Reason *replaced* God. You don't go *back* to God after the Renaissance crowd, and all on down to the Romantic poets, told Him to kiss our butt. Hell, I were Him, or Her, I wouldn't talk to us neither. Besides, you know what Kierkegaard's dying words were. Pal, I blew it. I shoulda married that Frieda chick. Safe sex is the answer. Solves nothing, hurts nobody, and ya ain't hung-over the next morning."

"I ain't bonding with you, Gus."

"Well you don't exactly blow my party favor either, big F., uniform or no uniform."

"Gus, you know what I think? I think we're *beyond* absurdity. Being absurd meant thinking there might still be a moral order in the universe. You seen anything lately resembling moral order? Only now, we're *beyond* worrying about it, too. Moral order was an illusion. Now we got the TV. Down the road, something else'll come along. Or it won't. *Que sera sera*, compadre."

"Pretty laid back view, Festus."

"Yeah well, that Prozac's one damn fine medication."

"Think there's a Hell?"

"I figure if there are forty billion solar systems and we ended up on a planet as fucked up as this one, this is Hell. We're the mutant race. Screw up somewhere else, ya get sent here to be human."

"It ain't all bad."

"Oh, I know. That's what makes it so dang terrible."

"Reckon there's an afterlife?"

"That which has been is now, and that which is to be hath already been."

"So, kind of an eternal moment thing?"

"If you gotta hang a name on it."

Gus ponders a while. "Maybe the leap of faith don't have to be religious. You know, if we're in despair maybe we need a comic leap, seeing things as funny so we's can cut bait on all the sentimental hypocrisy that passes for meaning in the world."

"I ain't in despair."

"Well you're medicated. Your feelin's is right up there with silicone implants. You got an emotional life that's about as real as a rubber boob."

"That hurt, Gus."

"Aw…shoot, Festus."

As the sun sets on the oil-darkened bay, only the lap of the waves, the rustle of medical waste washing ashore, and the lulling, rhythmic boom of fighter jets bombs can be heard.

"So this is dying?" Sheriff Dave says. "The final dimming of the bulb, the last flicker of electric candlelight. And it arrives here, on the floor of a ramshackle bait shop. You been a good friend, Gus."

"You too, Festus."

"Whatcha' thinking about?"

"Crystal Goodlay. Man, she sure was purty. What you thinking about?"

"How I'd like to come back in the next life as a protagonist."

"Think it'd be any better?"

"Heck in high heels, G.C.! It's gotta beat wanking your jackson over a swimsuit calendar while other guys get the babes."

"Festus, I think you seen the light."

#

Lust, Lost and Found

'Twas not quite another formulaically dark and stormy night at the evil merchandiser's hilltop production plant, more like a milky gray smog, what with all the car fumes rising through headlight glow to strip the sleepy bayside hamlet of its ozone layer. The TV is tuned to the Elvis Channel, its "Watch Your Butt" weather warning displayed in the screen's lower left corner, obscuring 25% of "Clambake" as it predicts possible thunder, hail, tornadoes, and flooding from global warming.

But the profit-focused madman is too distraught to note the

evening's mucky turpitude. He paces the castle's fiberglass enclosed parapet, hair aglow and shinier than his silk bathrobe, which sways above his Birkenstocks and crew socks like a Roman emperor's tunic. Except, Dr. B's designer toga bears his initials, T.(he) E.(vil) Dr. B., Ph.D., in banana yellow thread manufactured specially from genetically altered silkworms to match strands of the craven zillionaire's hair.

"Oh, woe wis me," cwies da pwuague-meister, resorting to his Elmer Fudd imitation in order to mitigate the depths of his grief. For in one hand he holds—no, not a Bud Lite, that's the other hand—the kiss-off note from ex-femme fatale and aging underwear goddess Crystal G., soon to be Princess Goodlay and baby incubator royale.

"My dark Knight," her missive begins, and the sight of the supermodel's handwriting brings a single tear or leakage of Visine to the doctor's eye. He didn't think she could sign anything but her name, let alone allude to medieval quest literature. (Or maybe she's referring to "Star Wars," as in Jedi knight. Hm?) Evidence of a mind in the supervixen's uncluttered noggin causes our jilted suitor to pine all the more theatrically. He chugs his nearly frozen and tasteless brewski, belches, then in his despair forgets to recycle the can. He reads on.

"Forgive me, but I must to a more determined plow submit my still fertile, but ignominiously barren field. The clock ticks. I, nay none that dare call herself, or, okay, himself, human can stay the hand of time. Too soon my once pearl-like eggs will begin dropping irregularly, bearing all the vitality of roasted chestnuts. Hence, while ripeness remains and blush out of a bottle yet passes for the bloom of nature's hand upon my cheekbones, I must in sorrow surrender my nubility for nobility, before my boobs have to be supported by Ionic columns.

"Don't hate me, darling. The time I spent with you was the happiest I've ever been cloning viral DNA. But you have a doctorate, Philip has a fiefdom. Alas, it may seem retro of me to covet something so quaint as a title. (Now you'll have to call me Lady Goodlay, you bad boy.) And I know I must sound like some bitch out of Restoration comedy. Nevertheless, as global corporations set up feudal economies based around manorial production sites staffed by eight dollar an hour serfs, betrothal to the drone who would be king appears, on second glance, positively apropos.

"Oh, Horatio, I know you'll rule a fat-free world one day. And I wouldn't trade the stock options in InfoSic, Inc. you gave me for all the tech stocks in China. Still, a woman's heart grows impatient. Boys quest, girls nest. I've seen the world, mostly in skimpy underwear. Now I just want to stay home in my castle with my babies and five hundred servants.

"So adieu, my evil genius. (Not that I won't be suing you for palimony payments before my nups. But I'll let the royal barrister harass you about that. I'll tell him not to make your life too miserable, my sweet).

"Formerly yours, and now Princess in more than just attitude, C.G."

The lovelorn mad scientist holds the letter's legal stationery to his nostrils and inhales, hoping for a sinusful of Crystal's lingering scent. But all he gets is a whiff of her mass market discount brand of perfume, Cheap Date. "Not even the good stuff," he moans, crumpling the note, along with her lawyer's demands for profit-sharing in all products and intellectual property conceived, created, wondered about, or what-iffed by the always industrious corpo-patenter of all things fat-free and informationally viral in the presence, corporeal, virtual, imagined, or otherwise, up to and including longings for Crystal during her absence, of the ex-supermodel, pursuant to the plaintiff's shacking up with der Prince.

Horatio flings the summons into his personalized smoker where, at this very moment, the brisket and ribs he has been sweating begin to smell better than Crystal ever did. He forks a rack of pork onto a paper plate, grabs another cold one from the ice chest, and settles down at the parapet's picnic table with sauce, pickles and a little light reading.

But what's this?! Some fiend has slipped a copy of an internationally famous men's magazine in with the good doctor's subscriptions to *Chemical Compounds Today*, *Imperialist Quarterly*, the latest Batman comic (maybe this is the dark knight C.G. meant, being privy to the evil virus creator's juvenile fixation with the caped and obviously homosexual crusader?), plus his complimentary copies of *Shape*, *Trim*, *Skin & Bone* and *Fat No More*. Munching on a rib, the relentlessly inquisitive genius succumbs to studying the effects of low body fat on the female anatomy in the men's monthly when—Holy Boner, Batman!—his contact-lensed peepers alight on the not so discreetly parted lab coat and highly polished cowboy boots of sexual succulence personified, and holder of the "Girls of Campuses by the Interstate" crown for "Best Bum," Naomi, the soon to be damsel in distress, and girl without a last name.

"Her buns can sandwich my brisket anytime," croons the arch capitalist, who seems to suffer from a romantic version of Alzheimer's, because Princess Goodlay is instantly royal history. He immediately rings his English butler by cellular phone.

"Malaprop, prepare the (dare he call it the Bonesmobile?)…the minivan."

"Immutably, my lord."

"And how in the—"

"The men's publication, sire? My suspiration is that some concerned mansavant instilled it anon your more scientological papers, your grace." Having traversed the castle floors, Mal materializes upon the parapet where the dynamic duo now carry on their phone conversation within a rib's length of one another.

"Well, shucks, that's mighty thoughtful of you, Mal."

"No one understudies the suffrage of solitaire like a butler, my liege. May I inquest as to the object of your erection?"

Horatio fingers the photo image of the surnameless Na.

"Dialectical, sire."

"Convenient, too. She lives only down the hill."

And so, with scarce another word, evil and its minions are out of the garage and at the castle gate, awaiting Reefer's reacquaintance with consciousness. The minivan's horn startles the unshaven security guard and his whiskered companion Killer, and the pair bolts upright on the guardhouse couch in front of reruns on the Cartoon Network.

Vanside, man and canine salute their employer. "Playing possum," chuckles the hemp advocate. "Say, y'all going out?"

"Just open the frigid gate!" chastens the butler.

Then the van speeds off, leaving the suddenly hungry security team alone and curious. Reefer sniffs the hickory-smoked air. Killer is instinctively way ahead of him, tail awag. "Something sure smells mighty suspicious out on the parapet. What say we take a little security tour?"

"Woof!"

#

Ideological Misgivings, Ghosts, and an Invitation in the Form of a Cliché

Following Naomi's kidnapping, my choices were simple.

I could steal a Navy Frogman's suit, enter the castle's piranha filled moat after dark, scale the sheer wall of the home-office tower Naomi was being held captive in, penetrate its motion sensitive security system, demolecularize myself in order to pass through the unbreakable bay window that prevented Naomi from escaping the cell-like office cubicle (which had a pretty nice view of the theme park actually), cut the silk bonds chaining her to the serial computer she was expected to process information at, divest her from her shares in InfoSic's profit sharing plan, and then calculate and pay the short term capital gains tax (and probably interest and penalties for not filing estimated) on profits from shares the evil mogul had used to lure her away from college loans and dreams of veterinary school in order to work for him.

Or, I could find a new girlfriend. I mean, how hard had it been the first time? If Romeo and Juliet had gone to college, they would have been like, "Don't you think we should see other people... temporarily?"

If information had rendered meaning meaningless, mass culture had replaced true love with choice. Tristan vowed to go to hell for Isolde, but what were his options? Date the sheep farmer's daughter if she promised to shave her mustache? I can slide over to the coed weight room and eyeball more A-1 booty in one workout than the Knights of the Round Table saw on fifty grail quests.

But, epic questers traditionally want what they can't have, mainly the grail cup, immortality, and the king's significant other. So I was bound by legend to snatch Na from the evil CEO's castle.

Only, if I rescued Naomi just because she had one of the three best butts on the planet, I'd be guilty of sexist elitism. Is beauty truth; or a commodity with a high sticker price?

I was forced to consider a Marxist-feminist interpretation of my heroic dilemma. According to their ground rules, I was to subvert my quest, forsake Naomi to the velvet claws of capitalistic evil, and marry a homely but kindhearted carpentress who pounded nails for the Habitat for Humanity. This sounded noble. But free market capitalism doesn't appreciate noble.

So, since the best relationships are based on trust, I thought it only fair to apprise Na of my concerns by e-mail.

To: Naomi-the-coveted@maidenhood.com
"Dearest Na,
"I know you're in captivity (♀), but I'm working on springing you. Trouble is, being postmodern, I'm ambivalent about the authenticity of heroic action in a pluralistic mass culture. Heroism to me might be gender imperialism to you.

"Let's say I do storm the castle and rescue you from the clutches of evil. Are you going to like being eternally indebted to me? As a feminist you should be resourceful enough to escape on your own. Unless, of course, you don't want to escape because being the concubine of a mega-rich fascist has placated all your feminist ranting about equality. Maybe you want to be Eva Peron, I don't know. I just don't want to come crashing in like Lancelot, then get reamed for objectifying you.

"Of course, if I *don't* try and rescue you, you're going to be pissed too. So I'm kind of like, what *do* you want? Self-empowerment, or continued deification by a male value system?

"Because I respect your individual rights to construct your own identity, I'm heroically paralyzed. The decision's up to you. Let me know what you think. I can go either way.

"Signed,
"Possibly your one true love and potential liberator. Or, subjugator; it depends on how you see things.

Will@epicqwest.com"

But when I clicked "send," a new command appeared on Spunky's screen.

"Before we @InfoSic Systems can process your electronic transmission, we are delighted to offer you the services of the world's leading cybersecurity systems at no charge. To receive the service, as well as free links to other Web sites in the InfoSic universe, simply enter your name, Social Security, driver's license number, date of birth, preferred credit card, and the seven letter security code of your choice."

Ostensibly a hero, it remained my job to resist evil in every form until such time as evil and capitalism became indistinguishable. So I typed, "Fuck you."

"We're sorry. That code is redundant. Please choose another seven letter password."

"Privacy."

"We're sorry."

"Meaning."

"Please try a—"

"Consume."

"Thank you. Processing your transmission. While you're waiting, perhaps you'd like to browse our online mall. Please enter your current interest."

"Epic quest."

An image of a hiking boot morphed onto the screen. "These durable and stylish footwear accessories … "

Obviously my rescue of Naomi was going to include some impulse buying.

Yet, no word came. My plea for direction went unanswered. Only unsuggestive silence emanated from my e-mail port, as if Naomi suddenly thought she was God.

In the quad, I stood under a smog-mottled sky and was about to howl at the heavens in existential despair when someone handed me free concert tickets and some instantly classic coupons from Madman Pizza. "You'd have to be crazy to order from anybody else," it read, above a picture of Charles Manson. They were ideal for my collection. I was like, cool. Then I chastised myself for being so easily distracted from my quest, but that lasted about three seconds.

To whom could I turn for guidance? What was said in the humanities building about human existence was cancelled across the promenade by what was said in the physical sciences building. Then all of it was collected as paradox in what would have been a library, if the building had had any books in it, or rendered useless the instant it hit the administration building.

The world, I saw, was a Pandora's box of information. And, as information multiplied, humankind's wisdom and authority shriveled. Maybe quests no longer end in enlightenment, but in confusion. In the beginning was the Word, in the end words, words, words.

And here, at my lowest ebb, my guidance counselor tapped me on the shoulder with a seven iron—perhaps the most versatile of clubs. When I turned, there hovered his suntanned visage like Hamlet's father's ghost back from a golf vacation.

"Will, gotta tell you something. All this questing after knowledge is great. Heck, it's what a university-by-the-interstate's for. But, you know, a pretty sharp old Greek guy once said, the quest for knowledge often overlooks the necessity of applying the knowledge gained to the life you're living. Now I'm just a geezer, but I say you go after the girl."

He lowered his head and languidly swung the seven iron, then watched an imaginary ball arc and hop onto an equally ineffable green. "Ooo! Almost birdied it. Anyway, you're surrounded here by some of the finest minds on our tiny and inexplicably interstate-bound peninsula." Then he leaned close and whispered, "Although, just between you, me and the Coke machine, eggheads sure can drain the primal vitality out of a guy."

A fighter jet roared by overhead and my reincarnated guidance counselor pointed at it with his number seven.

"Heck, you think those hot dogs'd stop to dwell on the niceties of postmodern ideology if Naomi was their main squeeze? Shoot, that hilltop laboratory'd be smoking like a grilled sausage. So, as your guidance counselor, I counsel you to get the old testosterone pumping."

"I thought you were dead."

He paused in mid-swing. "Now what Ph-ilosopher D-ope went and planted that lamebrain idea in your head?"

"Your doppelganger character, the sheriff, died on the floor of Old Man Cotter's ramshackle bait shop three chapters ago.

He felt his chest with his hands, then handed me his golf club and told me to take a swipe at him. "Dang," he said, after the iron passed through the apparition masquerading as his head. "Maybe I'm like one of those guardian angel characters sent to watch over you. You know, innocent but wise."

"You don't think you could be an epileptic hallucination?"

"Are you taking your medication?"

"Yeah."

"Well, then I'm probably real."

"Real?"

He conked me on the head with trusty *numero siete*. "Yeah, as in ouch."

He had a point.

And so, for advice on plotting the conclusion of my quest, I once again sought out that arbiter of what passes for wisdom in our infomacracy. That tenured rebel, and author of the ultimate monograph on pomo cinema, "The Blockbuster as Ironic Behemoth."

"What in our hype-driven megaculture satisfies, even as it *subversively satirizes*, our collective desire for human solidarity along with our need to see things blow up more pointedly than the ..."

My film professor. Amazingly, he answered after only fifty attempts to reach him during his office hours. I explained my plight. His solution was instantaneous and totally Hollywood.

"Let's do lunch!" he shouted.

#

A Short, Disturbing Chapter

After he'd given me directions on where to meet him, I rode the campus tram to its final stop, then walked past low rent condos that gave way to mobile homes and, finally, to the shacks I had always seen at a distance from the top floor of the Virology building. Signs for live bait, snakes, and auto repair were staked in patches of dirt, discarded souvenirs from the theme park scattered around them.

A young boy in a driveway stopped chucking rocks at a wheelless pickup truck and stared at me like I'd just arrived from the moon. When I waved, he waved back warily, as if to protect himself. And I knew then that he and I suffered from different strains of Information Sickness.

My strain informed me that I had lost all sense of meaning, his that he would live without any sense of hope. And neither of us said a word, as if the abyss between us was our dirty little secret.

#

Easy Writer

I think I was having a reaction to my seizure medication, because the sunlight reflecting off the hogs parked outside the biker bar seemed to coalesce into a ghostly message that read, "You are now entering Act III of your epic memoir."

"Absolutely," my film prof. said. He was wearing a Life Sucks, So Go To The Movies T-shirt. "Rescuing the girl is penultimate climax material according to the Universal School of Script Doctors bible, *Writing To Sell When You Have No Talent.*"

We were seated at a table waiting for our order of corn dogs and onion rings to be set on our plastic skull-and-crossbones placemats, while aging bikers settled arguments by hitting one another over the head with their walkers. All around me, leather jackets boasted Hell's Angels and AARP patches. The jalapeño burger on the menu was called "The Wild One" and came with a side of Zantac. I'd never been in a room before where so many people, women included, looked like Jerry Garcia.

"Now, there are a couple of key rules for Act III," he reminded me. "First, the girl must have great legs and be as scantily clad as possible. Ripping, shredding and tearing off of clothing during escape scenes is totally viable because somebody else out there already did it and made money. Sacrifice is a great device for getting rid of clothes. Say the imperiled group comes to a waterfall. There's no way down without a rope. She hesitates, out of modesty, then offers her jeans. The subtext is immediately richer."

"Who is this *asshole*?" Spunk howled.

I chuckled sheepishly and shrugged. "He's big on First Amendment rights."

"Chuckling sheepishly is good. A lame, but time-tested comic response to embarrassment and possible violence upon your person. You're the good-natured, level-headed buddy. Your laptop's the about-to-blow-his-cork half of the team. Temperamentally mismatched best friends, the odd couple as action heroes."

"Good?"

"Better than good—clichéd. Done to death. Because, I gotta tell you, Information Sickness still feels a little vague to me. Okay, you've got a virus that can be transmitted intellectually, abstractly, or by fat-free food. People read *People* and—whammo! They realize that all the military, entertainment, and business worshiping horseshit masquerading as information in the world has eclipsed meaning. Hype replaces purpose. Fat-substitutes replace food. So, people realize this and they ... what?"

"Rage, despair, die. Or, and I believe this is the more widespread symptom, they internalize the sickness so completely that they carry on as if nothing had happened. Only the emptiness of their lives in time comes to feel like they missed a chance to make a better world."

He threw an onion ring at me. "Great, a popcorn movie! What are you, fucking meshuggah?"

Apparently, he'd vaulted into L.A. speak—sound and fury signifying nothing by megalomania.

Information Sickness insight #11: the intellectually challenged always believe they know best.

"Look, let's go back to symptom one, rage. You, as the hero, embody the audience's rage against disempowering and boring pomo existence, personified by evil fat-free maven, and predatory chick snatcher supreme, Dr. B. He's threatening mankind. He stole your girlfriend. Plus, he concocted and disseminated the pernicious viral disease known as Information Sickness that stripped your mother's mortality of its dignity, and set you on the path to continually misdiagnosed and erroneously medicated comic despair. You know what chapter eight, article six of the Universal Script Doctor's bible demands that characters in your situation do?"

"Litigate?"

"Kick his ass!"

"How about a strong verbal condemnation of his actions?"

"*La mort!*"

And so, with a formulaic death warrant issued for the overpaid corporate fiend, my film professor gave me some matchless advice for concluding my epic memoir.

"Get out quickly, but slowly. Reek mayhem, but show compassion. Be funny, yet serious. Bittersweet, but happy."

"Black, but white."

"Exactly! And give me more of Mom. I like her. She's sort of this stoic, loving, wise…"

"Antithesis to the ethically bankrupt men in the book?"

"Yeah! Bump that up. Only…"

I knew. Sentimental, but touching. Schmaltzy, but poignant. Intimate, yet commercial.

#

In Which the Prospect of Death Wonderfully Concentrates My Mind

This time my mother drove. I remember looking out the window and not saying much, and Mom let me stay inside myself as if, by instinct, she knew that was where I needed to be. The hospital wasn't covered with ice as we approached it this time. Somehow, without my noticing, spring had crept over the face of things again, revealing not the gray-brown tones of late March, but true spring, when what little is left of the natural world hums with color, shaming all we'd erected in its midst.

At the admissions desk, more information was sent ping-ponging through the world as my mother filled out forms for my EEG. The woman at the computer never looked at me, even to confirm what she read off the screen. After a few moments I began to feel that I wasn't validating the information, it was validating me.

When we were alone again outside the neurologist's office my mother said, "I don't know how we wound up here, sweetie."

She squeezed my hand and I looked at her fingers. What amazed me was not how beautiful or soft they were, because they weren't those things really. What amazed me was that they were there: my mother's fingers where there could have been nothing.

I know this recognition seems simple, maybe even dumb. If it is, so be it. I make no excuses. I am no longer mad to connect every effect to a cause. That the world is, that there is something instead of nothing upon nothing, *is* perhaps all we may ultimately call meaning. At least, as I held my mother's hand, this was all I felt I could claim to know. Yet, somehow, it felt right.

In her office, the neurologist we'd come to see neither agreed or disagreed with my psychopharmacologist(s)' guess that I suffered from seizure disorder.

"People have all kinds of seizures for all kinds of reasons," she told us. "*Deja vu* is a seizure, but it's confined to the temporal lobe. It doesn't spread to other areas of the brain. In other words, no biggie. You don't know anybody who's been hospitalized for *deja vu*, do you?"

"I think I would have felt like I remembered if I had."

"Hey," she said, lifting her pen and pointing it at me, "funny." She rolled her stool over to me so we were face to face. "Usually a symptom in the late stages."

"Bad?"

"It'll probably require full cranial replacement. What color hair you want with your new head?"

"Bleached blond."

"Open your eyes wide." She shined her penlight into each one and put her face close to mine. "He always such a jokester?" she asked my mother.

"When he isn't worrying."

"What are you worried about?" she said, then looked at me with that expression women of a certain age can conjure up, half-seduction, half-amusement at the triviality of your anxiety, as if they could whisk it away with a single kiss, and sate all your needs, erotic, metaphysical and maternal.

Staring at her, I felt I could almost articulate what had gnawed at me ever since my mother's cancer scare. But my mother spoke first.

"The meaning of existence."

"Oh." The woman nodded her head. "That little old thing. Yeah. See a lot of people about that." She began feeling my skull for, I guess, dents. "Any recent head injuries? Fall off a bike? Get beaned by a baseball?"

"No."

"Mom, did you drop him on his head a lot when he was a baby? Conk him on the noggin with frying pans? That kind of stuff."

"No."

"No. I didn't think so."

"Drink a lot of alcohol? Coming home trashed five times a week?" she asked me.

"No."

"Watch a lot of TV?"

"Some."

"Sit close to it? Right up on it."

"No. Normal."

"Sugar, nothing's normal. It's *all* individual. Any reactions to flashing lights? You know, in discos, places like that."

"Despair."

She sat back on her stool, her lips puckered around a smirk. "Okay, why don't you tell me what happened at the time of the reputed seizure."

I did.

"And were you taking Prozac and Haldol?"

"I'd kind of lost interest in medication by then."

"Why?"

I was silent.

"It's okay. Your mom knows you have a sex drive. Orgasms are a form of seizure, a very pleasant form." She exchanged glances with my mother. "At least from what I remember." Then she said, "Look, seizure disorder is very hard to pinpoint. First of all," she looked at my mother again, "it's *rarely* genetic. It is *rarely* inherited. What causes seizures? Any number of things. Head injury, alcoholism, medication—hm? Photo-sensitivity to bright lights or television patterns. Low blood sugar, sleep deprivation, tumor— *rarely*. Even a virus."

"Virus?"

"In about 3% of cases. The thing is, in 65% of cases we don't have a clue as to what causes a seizure. If you even had a seizure, which I'm not ready to claim you did. A seizure is a symptom of the brain reacting to internal shocks, or surprises. How the brain reacts varies from individual to individual. 'Spacing out' is a form of seizure. It all depends on your personal convulsive threshold. For some people it's high, for others… eh. So, why don't we go see if the EEG tells us anything."

She led us to an examination room where there was a bed, a gaggle of wires on its pillow, and a cart with a machine console at the foot of it.

"We're going to have you lie down, stick some electrodes here and here and here," she pressed her fingers to my skull as if administering a blessing, "then put you to sleep for a while since your brainwaves change when you're not awake. Okay?"

I nodded.

"Janey will be here in a minute."

My mother kissed me, her lips lingering on my brow. "How you doing?"

"I'm worried about the meaning of existence."

"It just slipped out. I'm sorry. Maybe this test will tell us something."

"Yeah, maybe they'll get lucky."

Janey arrived and held the door as a signal for my mother to leave, which, after kissing me lightly once more, she did. Then she was gone and it was my turn to be alone with whatever new information concerning my mortality science could deliver.

Janey measured my head from the bridge of my nose to the crown of my skull, then hummed while she brushed adhesive paste onto patches of my scalp and stuck silver wires to them. Small rubber caps affixed other electrodes. She asked me to lie back, turned on the machine, and injected me with a sedative that she told me would put me to sleep in twenty minutes.

Commands followed. Open your eyes, close your eyes. Breathe deeply, look at the flashing light. The feeling of having surrendered made me imagine—and maybe this was simply because I had begun to fall asleep—that I was dying. I felt layers of my body being peeled away. I don't know if this was how my mother felt on the operating table. We never talked about it. Dying, it seemed, went on in a hidden, unspeakable place.

When Janey's voice faded, I remembered the wires attached to my head. I wondered if they could send a message back to where I'd come from. Because, I wanted to know why we had ever imagined there could be rational meaning in a world where a son can't save his mother, a mother can't save her son, and each goes to their death alone, emptied by reason and information of all that might have given them peace.

And lying there half-awake, I felt adrift in a Lethe of information. And it told me that I, Will@epicqwest.com, had been demoted: from epic quester to cartoon hero. My mythic longings were a joke. My grail cup had a Coke logo on it.

But maybe this was necessary. Maybe to reincarnate meaning I had to stop taking *myself* seriously. If all is paradox, then what could more fully express human longing than a cartoon?

"Well," the neurologist said when I woke, "your brain waves don't show any spikes. No differentiation in pattern from right lobe to left lobe. If anything, I thought we might have seen a minor discharge, which is typical of *absence*, or *petit mal*. Seizures so brief you don't even recognize them. But, nothing. The next step is a CAT scan to look for structural abnormalities." She looked at me. "Feel like your brain's abnormal?"

"Nothing's abnormal. It's all—"

"Wise guy. Look, I don't think a scan is going to turn up anything. If you continue to have symptoms, then we'll get you under the camera. Otherwise, the episode was an anomaly, possibly brought on by your medication. We know a lot about the chemistry of the human brain, but sometimes we lose sight of exactly how much we *don't* know."

So, even medical science had succumbed to Information Sickness.

"What about my penis?" I asked.

She laughed. "What about it?"

"How long before my erections look like question marks?"

She lowered her puzzled face into my file. "You mean, Peyronie's disease? That's occasionally caused by Dilantin Kapseals. You're taking Depakone Capsules."

"Oh." Looks like somebody's voice technology software needed its electronic ears waxed.

My mother treated me to lunch on the way home. I was the one who was supposed to be physically, or perhaps mentally, endangered at the moment. But my mother looked beat. Ever since she'd hit forty her face could look ten years younger or older than it actually was in the course of twenty-four hours. A bad night's sleep and she aged a decade.

"I don't know what to do, Will. All we do is go around in circles." She was staring into that blank hole in the middle of the world five inches from everyone's face, that spot we turn to when we're out of answers but still looking for a solution.

And so, I could have stayed on my medication and continued reaching after facts about my "condition." Or, I could leave behind the circles reason and medical science spun us in and, as all questers do, try to rescue meaning from death, even if meaning had become mutable and fleeting, and quests as irrational and cartoonish as they were necessary.

If I had to battle Information Sickness and fat-free food instead of dragons, I would do so, I decided. After all, what really mattered? What psychiatry labeled me? Or what I could say I either did, or imagined I did, then heroically posted online, in the face of death?

#

The Butterfly Effect, or In Which My Quest Grows Unforeseeably Complex

"I think the answer to your question," ABD Chandra cooed, "is, how do you global pop merchants say, a no-brainer."

She had agreed to meet me at her apartment to discuss the seemingly chaotic nature of my quest. Also because she wanted company. "This is a very lonely country, your America. Don't people get out of their cars? I see them riding everywhere with their telephones and soft drinks. They order food through windows then eat it while driving aggressively. A street beggar doesn't stand a chance."

"We're kind of into self-reliance," I explained as she removed what looked like sunburned chicken from her oven. "You know, rugged individualism."

"I don't see anything rugged in crashing air-conditioned sports vehicles on holiday weekends." She began sautéing bananas in butter and spices. "I also don't understand your malls. People visit them to fondle products instead of talking to one another."

"We talk during 'quality time.'"

She spooned the bananas onto a plate and handed it to me. "Please garnish with those hand-picked herbs behind you. Very special. Grown myself."

"Legal?" I said, holding a pinch of the green stuff to my nose.

"Totally. And known to cure all manner of diseases."

"Really?" I scarfed a handful while ABD Chandra tossed rice pilaf. Five seconds later I understood the meaning of existence. Only I can't explain what it was because all I remember is flames shooting out of my nose.

"Good for the sinus passages," ABD said, after I'd wolfed my fifth gallon of iced tea.

We sat cross-legged at a low candlelit table. Linen napkins had been rolled and secured with delicate twig wreaths, the silverware so brightly polished that it threw glints of light around the room like a disco ball.

"Please to indulge," she said, pointing out each dish. "Tandoori chicken, pilaf, cucumber *rayta* to soothe the palate, banana *pakora vindalu* with, as you know, secret herb, *poori*, vegetable *samoosas* and, for dessert, homemade Washington bing cherry ice cream with hand-rolled profiteroles and bittersweet chocolate cream anglaise in hand-thrown majolica pots."

"That come with sprinkles?" I felt like Vishnu had been reincarnated as Martha Stewart.

"You cute boy. Eat. You look thin and pale. Then tell me how I may be of the utmost service to you."

"Well, I've decided to rescue Naomi from that profiteer of evil, Dr. B., no matter how pissed off she gets over my heroic interruption of her corporate captivity."

"Why would she, as you say, enter into a state metaphorically, and to me incomprehensibly, linked to urination? All girls wish to be rescued."

"I'm not sure if that applies to members of FWISM—Feminist When It Suits Me. Plus she lives in a billionaire's castle."

"Then I'm afraid you do have a dilemma. For, even exceeding a girl's desire for romantic adventure is the desire to decorate. Think of the opportunities a castle offers. Bab-Wallah!"

I scanned ABD Chandra's cozy garden apartment and noticed that it did resemble those checkout line magazine covers where furniture and rooms are too perfect for human occupancy. Not only was I up against rapacious evil, I had to take on the housewares industry as well.

"This is why you can help," I told her. "Since I'm facing an overwhelming array of postmodern obstacles, I thought complexity theory might be able to guide me toward the end of my quest."

"Certainly my input in this most delicate of areas will prove invaluable. But, first, isn't there something?..."

I had Spunk on the table and displaying "Print Preview" selections of her spellchecked and appendixed dissertation before she could say Ali Baba.

"Loyal and exceedingly responsible American friend! I am having waves of joy."

"I'm good to my friends when I need something from them."

"Soon you will be calling me Dr. Chandra. Or, as I am your intimate confidant, Doc for short." About to Be Dr. Chandra leaned across the table and planted a kiss on my lips.

"Nice lipstick."

"Thank you. It's curried. But, now in my cerebellum are dancing visions of how to thank you." She vanished and returned in a flash, veiled and barefoot. "Presto! Prepare to enjoy firsthand the ancient art of belly dancing."

She began to clap the tiny cymbal rings on her fingers, her hips undulating like a flesh sea inches from my face, and I knew instantly why Shaharazad had to beat off the Sultan with a stick. All-But-Dressed Chandra's skin had a dusky hypnotic radiance, and when she spun on her painted toenails to offer me a posterior view in observance of scientific thoroughness, the phrase "kiss my ass" surrendered all pejorative connotations. I felt transported. Somehow, Allah had made a living woman out of chocolate ice cream.

She turned again and shoved me to the floor, then stood over me, hula-hooping the mysteries of the East slowly down around my hips. It seemed that a performance was expected of me. Apparently Beaucoup-Desperate-Chandra, I realized, had been experiencing the great American loneliness in more than a cultural criticism sense.

Yes, I wanted to be faithful to Naomi. But as a truth seeker, wasn't I conveniently obligated to obey the truth of human biology? Being faithful to Na, who didn't even have the courtesy to drop a thank you note when I sent her a virtual bouquet of flowers by e-mail, meant betraying the laws of nature in order to obey a Western social construct. Guilt was a byproduct of information, hence a sickness.

Meanwhile, ABD (Anxiously-Begging-Deflowerment) Chandra continued to demonstrate the female anatomy's range of movement, causing a heroic response in the crotch of my pants by using a form of vulval massage unknown to Aryan girls. My reaction went beyond mere socialization, didn't it? It was sacred. Not making love at that moment to the world's leading unpublished authority on fractal virology would have been tantamount to spitting in the eye of God.

Anybody out there buying this?

ABDC clamped my nose between a pair of finger cymbals and pulled my lips to hers. "Simon Says, explore my palate with your tongue." It was clear AB hadn't renounced sexual desire on her path toward Nirvana. And, fortunately, Brahma had his A-team on duty the day ABD's earthly form had been reincarnated. She slipped my hands beneath her veils and pressed them around her buttocks. "Nice?"

"The stuff dreams are made of."

Then the world's most sex-starved virologist yanked my pants off, took me in hand and cried, "Open Sesame."

And I had to wonder. Maybe I was destined never to make love to Naomi. Maybe this was my fate. Maybe Western psychiatry and medication had my *karma* all screwed up, and my sexual encounters with Doc and Crystal Goodlay were my form of suffering. I was supposed to be in the celibate student phase. Instead, with the effects of my medication wearing off, I chose to use the lowest form of my *kundalini*, my life energy, to Kama Sutra my chaos theory connection.

"But, spontaneous choice is in the nature of complexity theory," Arundhati told me as we lay naked together on her Persian carpet. "Chaotic systems are, like life, dependent on minute variables that can occur spontaneously. Therefore, it is very difficult to predict their outcomes reliably. Like the weather. One molecule gets bumped by a butterfly and your five day weekend forecast goes out the window."

"You think that could be the trouble I'm having with my quest?"

"You have to understand something, we don't live in a Newtonian universe anymore. The universe is, in a classical sense, irrational. Straight-line geometry and classical physics never could explain complex behavior in physical systems. Quantum theory and fractal mathematics have now made this possible. So, if classical physics no longer holds, why would one expect a classic quest with evil subdued and virgins rescued to fare any better?"

"So it isn't hopeless? I just have to expect the unexpected."

"No, you have to *accept* the unexpected. Remember, surrender, too, is a victory. A victory of accepting what is, or what presents itself, over what one wants."

"That's un-American!" Spunk erupted, his Patriot-Check tool kit flashing. "I knew it. She's a spy. Why else would a schmuck like you get laid? I'm talking Mata Hari. Her nipples have probably been dipped in poison. She's got microphones in her cymbals. Naomi can hear every grunt!"

"True?" I asked her.

Arundhati's finger cymbals jingled as they landed in a far corner of the room. "A quester's strongest quality is his curiosity," she said, and then I knew the taste of victory when she presented her breast. Arundhati unclasped her hair and it fell around me, darkening the dim candlelight to a darkness that matched the ripe darkness of her body. As she slowly rose and fell against my hips, the rhythm began to feel as if it would continue forever, like the cycle of rebirth and suffering that was endlessly repeated, or the way the universe will collapse and explode anew, infinitely. How, then, could I renounce my desire, when the universe itself sprung out of desire, a desire to *be*? If Arundhati's nipple was poisoned, then its poison had the taste and glory of flesh. And as I lay there, anchored in darkness by her body, I felt as if I had floated up through the void made of human reason, left what I had once called meaning behind, and arrived, inexplicably, home.

"Our lovemaking is complexity theory in action," Arundhati whispered to me afterwards. "Who could have predicted that your coming here for quest advice would land us in what you Americans call the sack?"

"Who could have predicted that I'd have typed your dissertation?"

"You see. Unpredictable variables. Classical, straight-line physics cannot compute models for this behavior. Complexity theory has, however, discovered a formal elegance in the raggedness of the world. A beach may be beautiful, but it certainly isn't straight. Likewise, a quest may still be epic/heroic, but it might not climax in classical Aristotelian form. You know, here in the West, you are so convinced that good and evil are separate entities, like black and white. But look at our bodies." Our limbs were wrapped around one another like a braid of DNA. "Intertwined. Like good and evil. The two are one."

"So, no courtroom scene?"

"I wouldn't count on it, although it is formulaically popular. But complexity theory, like quests for meaning, cannot be OJ'd, just as human intelligence will never cede its authority to artificial intelligence, no matter how many Big Blues IBM pulls out of its relentlessly profitable hat."

"Who do you think fact-checked your dissertation?" Spunk wanted to know.

"Oh, you're a trusty little calculator, I'll give you that. But human consciousness is more than an abacus with a battery."

Spunk whined, "Will …."

"He's kind of sensitive," I told Arundhati.

"That's just a program. Spunky, I bet you don't know what a Fibonacci number is?"

"A series of numbers where each successive number is the sum of the previous two," the Spunkster announced proudly. "0,1,1,2, 3,5,8,13,21,34,55 …. Hahaha. Whee!"

While Spunk rattled off numbers, Arundhati stroked my chest. "See? Instantly forgotten. But humans are much more complex, particularly in matters of the heart. After all, we evolved by a series of accidents. Millions of years ago an infection occurred where prokaryotic cells that still exist today as bacteria and viruses became entangled with spirochetes, much as we are entangled now. The two bonded and the rest, as they say, is evolutionary history."

Arundhati snuggled against me and I wrapped my arm around her shoulders, something for which Naomi would never forgive me. Extra-curricular sex could be forgiven, like involuntary manslaughter. At nineteen, having spontaneous sexual liaisons was almost like killing in the line of duty. But unauthorized expressions of affection were the equivalent of murder one. Na would be able to prove intent.

Still, I didn't remove my arm. If human evolution had been made possible by the chaotic entanglement of two substances eons ago, the resolution of my quest might be no less fortuitous or accidental. And since when have epic heroes been reliable? Odysseus let down his sails at every grappa bar in the Aegean. Lancelot and Tristan cuckolded their king. Even Orpheus couldn't follow a simple rule, like don't turn your head if you ever want to get slippery with your girlfriend again. The illusion that epic heroes were ever in control was just that, an illusion. Fairy tales for the meaning-starved.

And there it was! The antidote to Information Sickness suddenly as clear to me as Spunky counting out, "10,816, 17,501, 28,317 ... " and Arundhati's latest temptation.

"And now, homemade Washington bing cherry ice cream?"

Hey, a hero has to eat.

#

Emerging Microbes, Emerging Markets

I was at home considering how to deploy my antidote when the doorbell rang.

"Son!" my father's voice rang out, with an enthusiasm that led me to suspect he'd just been licensed to mint money. The man standing beside him in the doorway seemed to have $$ signs for eyeballs.

I could see my antidote to Information Sickness would have to wait.

"You're out of jail," I said.

"Conviction rightfully overturned. If I'm a corporate scam artist, your mother's Princess Di." He peered into the living room. "Speaking of same, she or Roger Reject around?"

"They're both at work."

"Solid middle class values. Glad to see it." He stepped past me and his suited cohort followed. "Heard through the registrar's office that you've taken some kind of leave."

I closed the door and headed back to my bedroom. Dad sat at the foot of my bed as if he were going to read me a story the way he did when I was five. The man with the briefcase pulled over my desk chair.

"Fine," my father said. "School is for the unambitious. Did Bill Gates finish college? Did Shaq?"

Whenever my father wanted me to like him, he announced that he approved of my actions. Had I promised not to hate him for screwing my mother out of alimony payments, he would have said "good plan" if I told him I planned to blow up the Vatican.

"School is the biggest brain drain on the free market since the Manhattan project," his associate said. "People who could be employing the latest computer skills at lower wages than the microgeneration of workers preceding them are, instead, pointlessly chained to study carrels where they're brainwashed by humanities texts. It's a scandal of national proportions and I salute your rejection of it."

I understood what was going on without the benefit of a heroic revelation. It was simple. Women gathered around me when I needed care. Men arrived when they smelled profit.

"So, I think I can diagnose why you're laying up in bed in your bathrobe at two in the p.m.," my Dad said.

"While the market's still open," his pal added.

"Things have gotten complex. I'm thinking them over," I told them.

"Psychobabble! Those shrinks your birthgiver packs you off to can dispense the pills, all right."

"That's the one thing they're good for."

"But they know dick about the life force. The real happy drug."

"They wouldn't recognize it if it popped out of a straitjacket and bit them on the ass."

My father placed a hand on my leg and leaned closer. "Son, man is a maker. Okay? He makes things. Foremost, things like himself." My father paused, pretending he hadn't rehearsed this a million times. "Children, for example. The way I, and I suppose I have to let your mother into the equation, made you. But we make other things, too. Extensions of ourselves. Tools, products. I'm not going to tell you, Will, that we do this because it's good. Would you believe me anyway if I did? No. You know better. Man makes things because there are things to be made. Simple as that. We don't concern ourselves with good or evil. Just with production. Making. You can't moralize about Man's instinct. If idle hands are the devil's workshop, what hands made chemical weapons? What hands chopped down rain forests, or killed off ninety percent of plant, animal, and insect species on the earth? You see? We make things in the moment at hand. To us, the future is another world. The full range of implications concerning what we do at any given moment is too …" He floundered.

"Complex?"

"Exactly! Too complex to predict. We're here now, the future will be here later."

"That's the way it usually works," I reminded him.

"Right! See? We're connecting."

"Connection," his associate said. "Father and son. The chemistry's there. It's a natural."

"So, given the complexity of the present's relation to the future, we have to make what we can at the moment, with what we know at the moment, of the opportunities that present themselves at the moment, in the hope—"

"Hope," his partner echoed.

"—That what was useful at one moment might benefit—"

"Benefit."

"—Or illuminate some longstanding human purpose down the line. And, to see you lying here in bed on a day when God saw fit to put the sun in the sky—"

His crony interrupted and whispered in my father's ear.

"On a really nice day," my father continued, his pitch retailored to pander to his current audience, "well, I look at that and I have to say to myself, Will has lost his sense of purpose."

"Purpose."

"He has lost his desire to make things, to create. He has lost, and excuse me for saying it, the thing I named you for. Will. The doer, the maker."

"The destroyer?" I added.

"But destroying is part of making! Destroying clears the way for the new! If man didn't destroy, we'd still be enslaved to superstition and magic. Instead, we've freed ourselves to act as creators. And if you reject this part of yourself, Will, you destroy your old self without creating anything new in your place."

"Sad," his associate moaned. "Sadness personified."

"But," Dad said, taking a folder out of the briefcase, "it doesn't have to be this way."

"Nope."

He wiggled the folder. "What we've got here is…"

"Dynamite."

"A chance to create something. To create something useful. To create something…together. We think," he indicated his partner and himself, "that you're onto something with this Information Sickness business."

If he'd gonged my head with a sledgehammer I'd have been less stunned. "You believe me?" I said.

"Let's just say, what I believe isn't at issue here."

"You're the point man," the suit beside him said. "You're into all this kid world stuff that's beyond the ken of venture capitalists like myself. When your father told me about this in the mess hall—"

"You were in prison together?"

"It was a great sorting out period," the man confessed instantly, as if being a criminal had been a tremendous learning experience. "My priorities are stacked neater than the Bill of Rights. And we think Information Sickness could be the next Attention Deficit Disorder syndrome. You know, physiologically undetectable, no known cause, yet widely diagnosed. If a ten year old doesn't turn in his homework one day, he has ADD."

"A fad," my father said, "like recovered memory."

"It was like a toy. Parents wanted to be able to give it to their kids."

"Ritalin sales octupled."

"Likewise, if you mope for half an hour in December, you have Seasonal Affective Disorder."

"Roll out the Prozac."

"So, your dad and I think you're onto the next new thing."

"Sort of the viral equivalent of an MTV Buzz Clip."

"Viruses are very hot right now. Viral traffic, where viruses that have been around for millennia suddenly infect new hosts, is booming."

"We don't have to tell Will this," my father said.

"Hey, he's the specialist. What did I read, twenty words in *Time* magazine?"

"I failed Virology 101," I reminded them.

"But," my father assured me, "you understand what the sole purpose of a virus is, don't you?"

"Replicating itself."

"Is he a genius, or what?" his crony wanted to know.

My father nodded paternally, patting my leg. "Making more of itself. Right. Just like capital. Which is why we'd like you to take a look at this." He handed me the folder. Inside was a prospectus for a corporate start-up called ISN'T: Info Sickness Negation Technologies.

"ISN'T?" I said.

"As opposed to IS," my father said. "Information Sickness."

"Our stance," said the venture capitalist, "is that to exist in the information age *is* either to have Information Sickness, to be a carrier of Information Sickness, or to contain the genetic potential to develop either of the above."

"And we'd like to give technologically advanced humanity a chance to fight back," added my father. "Just like we talked about in the slammer, remember?"

I scanned the information. It read like biotech and psychopharmacological jargon copywritten by a New Age MBA.

"What we've come up with—" my father said.

"In a nutshell."

"—Is kind of a human V-chip technology."

"An agent that targets and eliminates information overload."

"Sort of an information immune system."

"An information vaccine. Synthetic cure for a synthetic disease."

"Can we ask Spunk to run some hypotheticals we've got here on disk?" Inserting it, Dad said, "How you doing, Spunk?"

"So-so. Will's been kind of withdrawn lately."

"Well, he's been sick, Spunk. But I think we've got him on the path to recovery now. Ready to crunch some numbers?"

"Abuse me. Really steam my chips."

Dad chuckled the phony chuckle of people who want something from you. Spunky's screen brightened. A collage of familiar images tumbled in and out of view—magazines, television, books, product labels, ads. "Information today," a voice destined to win a Worst Narration of an Industrial Film Award said, "surrounds us in a multitude of forms." Illustrations showed Joe and Jane Human walking through life, looking chipper and buying things. "But when information reaches dangerous levels of saturation," Joe and Jane were suddenly crushed beneath an avalanche of information, "happy, productive lives can turn to tragedy." Mall images faded into tombstones.

Then graphs demonstrated how an Information Sickness epidemic could impact consumer spending. "Consumers might actually begin to fear products," the narrator warned, "products that reach into every area of human life in order to deliver information."

My father's associate glanced at me, arching his eyebrows to indicate the dire yet lucrative situation Information Sickness offered us.

"At ISN'T, we have developed an information antibody that can act against Information Sickness the way Federal Reserve interest rate policy acts to halt inflation and fine tune economic growth."

"I love this part," my father said, as projections tracing the rise of IS, and a mutual decline in consumer spending deep into the new millennium appeared.

"You're sure about this?" I asked him.

"They're only estimates, but our confidence in them is high to high-plus. Spunk, run the numbers."

Spunk's spreadsheet system laid out a table of ISN'T's start up costs. "Mostly R&D," my father explained. The spreadsheets displayed hypothetical returns on investment, and calculated price to earnings ratios for ISN'T stock at one, three, five, ten and twenty-five year horizons. A dollar invested today, the figures claimed, would be worth two thousand dollars in two and a half decades.

"That's Dell, Intel, Microsoft territory!" Spunk crowed.

"It just makes sense, Spunk," my father assured him. "More information delivery systems in the world, more information in the world. More information, more Information Sickness."

"Sweet."

"And, we don't think a return of 2000% is out of line with our risk."

I didn't mention that their only "risk" seemed to involve sitting on the edge of my bed, talking.

"Does the return include reinvesting all dividends?" Spunk double-checked.

My father put on his "good question" face for the grim task of bringing more disappointment into the world. "Spunk, we don't believe a dividend is in the shareholder's best interest. We just want to take those profits and plow them right back into the company."

"Dividends," his associate chuckled. "What a kidder."

The three of them shared a laugh. Then I was informed as to how I would be exploited.

"You give us street credibility," Dad's partner suggested. "I mean, you actually went crazy from this stuff."

My father silenced his associate with a hand signal. "Will," he said, "I want to take you along with me on this, get you back on track. Here's a chance for you to jump into the exciting world of corporate virology without wasting five years getting a degree."

"No student loans to pay back, either."

"Look, we know that human immune cells *recognize* specific viral antigens, and leave friendly, healthy cells alone. So, we have to … finalize, or perfect, our product's genetic recognition system. Otherwise, our antidote won't be able to halt Information Sickness. Now, in order to effect this genetic … let's call it a genetic change of mind, first we need a specimen of the Information Sickness virus. Then we need to transfer this new genetic information into existing cells. Wait, let me clarify that: into existing *brain* cells."

"And the cutting edge method to effect this transfer," his partner assured me, "is by injecting genetically engineered viruses into a living brain."

"We don't totally understand the technology."

"We know fuck-all about the technology."

"But we're assured it's the most effective way to penetrate the brain's blood barrier, and relatively safe."

"Hey," Spunk offered, "no pain, no gain. This deal is logic city. I say we go for it."

So I was to be sacrificed, an offering to the marketplace. The god of venture capital had spoken, and my father had a scalpel at my forehead faster than insider trading moves an over-the-counter price.

I considered letting them have my brain, if that was what they wanted. It was a reasoning machine, the Spunkster with wig, only now it was so far gone in its ability to calculate, and thereby betray itself, that its concerns scarcely seemed any longer human.

"I'm already a psychopharmacological Frankenstein," I said. "Now you want to infect what's left of my brain?"

"Oh no no no no no."

"No."

"We just need some … "

"Help."

"A..."

"Partner."

"You see," Dad said, "we not only need a specimen of the virus from someone infected by it to perfect our antidote. We also know that an antidote to Information Sickness is only viable if there's a *boom* in Information Sickness. Well, we'd like assurance that there will be."

"That sicko's got your girlfriend!" his partner injected. When I looked at him, he shrugged. "Hey, venture capital does its homework."

"So we thought," my father continued, "okay, here's something we can bring to the table. Here's something *Will* can negotiate with."

"A piece of the action for Bones. He makes a buck spreading the disease, then a buck curing it."

"We offer him a stock swap. So many shares of IS, for so many shares of ISN'T. You're out of there with your girlfriend in twenty minutes."

Being categorically beyond disbelief at this point, I had no trouble accepting that my epic quest was about to culminate in a meeting. I'd be rescuing Naomi by corporate merger.

"That's it?" I said. "That's all you want?"

"Well, now that you mention it."

"You know those R&D lab guys and their kooky tests?"

They sure liked laughing together at things seemingly beyond their control.

Then they removed a syringe from the briefcase and drew blood.

"Kooky," the vampire capitalist said, staring at the specimen.

"Son," said my dad.

#

Fractal Finale: Or, The Uncertainty Principal Effect in a Quantum Quest

I had nothing to wear the day of my quest's climax.

"Nope," Spunk said disapprovingly when I tried on the imitation designer label suit I owned. "Too conventional, not to mention tacky. Think of how that's going to look next to Bones' get up. The guy has *eyebrows* by Armani. You're a quester, an outsider. You haunt the margins of history and myth."

I stepped into ripped jeans and pasted tattoos on my arms.

"Ooh, I'm terrified."

"Well, the outsider look is mainstream!" I snapped at him.

"I know somebody who thinks they don't need their medication," he sang.

I examined an old Halloween costume, which looked like pajamas with muscles drawn on. The superheroes I'd admired in my youth had been mutants, their superpowers blossoming from their flaws, their crime-fighting success a matter of accident. Like Space Cadet Boy, who bored criminals to death by never completing a sentence. Somehow, the idea of a superhero whose actions illuminated some moral purpose in the world seemed as dated as the rotary phone. So I returned the costume to its corner of the closet beside my old baseball, football and basketball uniforms. Then I took down the remaining rock star posters taped to my bedroom walls. I even untacked the Crystal Goodlay calendar I'd brought home from my dorm room, trashing all the false gods before me. If meaning no longer could be rescued by heroic action, I'd seek it stripped down to what I was—a Will without a plan.

"I'm ready," I said, back in my bathrobe.

"You're going like that?"

"Why not? Bathrobe Boy, the superhero who's always ready for bed."

My mom's Steed was in the shop, so I had to ride to my climax on the tram. If I may strike a plaintive note on the matter of all I realized mankind has lost in the way of myth, I will admit that as we passed the theme park I couldn't help but look upon it without wishing that I was approaching its faux castles to skewer Dr. B. like a kabob, then gallop off into heroic bliss, Naomi clinging to me tightly and, I suppose, Spunk flapping against the stallion's flank in the saddle bag. Who wouldn't?

But even two hundred million dollar movies can't sustain outmoded heroic illusions. You just can't keep throwing technology at emptiness. All you wind up with is FX signifying nothing; chaos without possible pattern.

You see, after the evening with Arundhati, I realized that I needed to move on to a search for fractal meaning. For the ragged, indeterminate, multiple truths of the world. Even if this meant facing down evil in my bathrobe, armed only with a venture capital prospectus. And so, perhaps the evolution of the hero does have to pass through cartoon. To go forward, leave old forms behind.

Anyway, I didn't have two hundred million dollars. My net worth was my pizza coupon collection and *Playboy* archive.

"Dead Week," the time students prepared for finals, had emptied campus. All the advertising signage beckoned as hysterically as ever, only, with no one around to tempt or badger, it seemed hollow. The food court stood empty, the mall shops and Cineplex, the parking lots, too. Empty. Construction had stopped on the International Volleyball Institute due to the latest inept scandal headlined on a copy of the student paper. "Imported Sand Administration Hoax. Toxic Bay Sand Used Instead." Only the "Caution: Biohazard" machines whirred to indicate the residue of a life form. The place felt unrecognizable to me, as if my medication had finally washed out of my system and, seeing things anew, I found myself standing in a cemetery of capitalism. Then a fighter jet tore a seam in the sky, its updraft rattling the frame shacks across the bay, and I knew I was only a ghost walking among echoes of what I'd once called home.

All quests end once the hero realizes there is nothing more to know, nothing more to be done. And I knew this. Because of the sickness? Perhaps. But as I passed the guardhouse, Reefer was gone, as I knew he would be, abandoning it for some other temp job. Killer had vanished too, as if the castle that once needed protection had mutated into something so vast and commonplace that insurrection or violence against it seemed laughable.

The evil Dr. B. would be gone as well. Yet, as profitably invisible as he always had been. There would be no anachronistic duel to the death between us. I would not chase him along castle parapets, scale down its walls with ropes I'd cut free with my sword, or battle him on the polluted bay's heath until, finally, I pummeled him into submission with my laptop.

Nor would there be the chance to let the Spunkster's legal ware system grill him about Information Sickness in a court of law. "Isn't it…(Could I even use the word ISN'T any longer, or did I need corporate approval?)…isn't it true you've patented fat-free substances capable of spreading like a virus, thereby desensitizing the human taste for meaning? If food is no longer 'real' but only a simulacrum of its original state, isn't it then only a matter of time before meaning, the thing humans generate out of the 'reality' of their existence, becomes a simulacrum of its original state as well? Haven't you, in fact, Doctor, in your pursuit of profit stripped humankind of its appetite for the truth?!"

No, none of that either. No judge would silence Spunk with an "Order in the Court!" My psychopharmacologist(s) would not be called to the stand to label me insane. Nor would that sellout Mr. Philosophy testify as an expert witness on the nature of meaning.

We were beyond that. Not just me, all of us. A fact Naomi, who was gone too, confirmed on the disk I was handed by Dr. B.'s attorney, once I had been shown into his office.

"Dear Will," I read off Spunk's screen.

"I hope you can understand the reason why I'm leaving you. It isn't just because Horatio bought the bastard network that cancelled my sitcom, which is now about a beautiful but sensitive girl who wants to save animals. You see, you never really knew me. I'm not a vain social climber. Think of me more like a subatomic particle, so delicate that your slightest gaze changed who and where I was. I hate to bring Heisenberg's Uncertainty Principle into breaking up with you, but the more you observed me, the more unknowable I became. Had we stayed together twenty years, we'd wind up perfect strangers to one another, like our parents.

"You're too precious to me to ever allow that to happen, Will. I'll never forget that you trashed your principles to get me an A. Life is full of surprises. It's like a cloud, constantly changing! And now, if you don't have a yucky brain tumor and can stay off anti-psychotics, you're free to change along with it.

"But, no matter what happens, we'll always have something special. Think of it. You're the only boy or man I'll ever have been in bed with and didn't screw. Unrequited love! Oh, Will, it's so romantic.

"You'll always be in my heart. Spunk too!

A zillion wet kisses,
Na"

"A zillion?" I muttered.

The attorney shrugged. "Used to be a million. Inflation. You have, I understand, a package for me."

I surrendered the prospectus, an act that, as Arundhati said, did feel like victory. And something more. I felt as if I were shedding an old life, becoming unborn. And, in that fluid zone between incarnations, I believed I could feel, like a blind man touching the features of a face, the contours of the new being I would become.

Scanning the numbers, the attorney said, "We'll get back to you on this. It has promise." Then, as magically as he'd appeared, he vanished.

Did my father merge with Dr. B? I imagine so. That kind of thing goes on all the time. But I don't think of either of them much anymore, and I imagine they, too, will vanish in time. All things do.

I don't respond to my psychopharmacologist(s) urgings to make an appointment, or stop posting my memoir online, either. None of them any longer has anything to do with me.

Did I fail in my quest? Maybe. Depends on how you look at it, and I'm looking at it from a new place. You see, the thing I realized that night at Arundhati's was that philosophy could no longer provide a single truth, just as quests can no longer offer hope of a single, ineluctable victory. They never had. They had only offered different illusions of truth and victory for a while. And, now, it was time to dismantle the singular quest into microquests. To scatter meaning into new, and perhaps at first, seemingly random patterns.

The day I left the hilltop laboratory, I came home, as I said, to die. To let my old form die, I mean. It's dead already, in fact. It died when I learned that beauty, not information, would save the world. As for how I'll resurface, in what new form capable of containing reborn meanings, I can't say right now. Only, I know it will be all right, because it will be whatever comes to be. The fractal future. The unpredictable now. The raggedly beautiful *is*.

And, actually, surrendering my old self bore fruit. For just when it seemed I might be alone, waiting for my new form to emerge, Arundhati appeared.

"I am with child!" she shouted. "I have a *chapati* in the oven! I am befetused!"

Which I, Will@epicqwest.com, will tell you was the best news I had heard in like ... forever. Information had once again been linked to meaning.

And so, now, as Arundhati and my mom prepare for the baby to come, I type.

"Do it," Arundhati said, after I told her I'd begun posting my epic memoir online. "I will bring home the *poori*."

I warned her that academic jobs were hard to come by.

"I am a foreign minority woman," she reminded me. "To academics, landing me will be like hitting the Trifecta. Those postcolonial wankers are going to pay through the nostril!"

The idea to record my quest had come to me one night as I lay in the dark with my head pressed to Arundhati's belly. I heard the beating of a heart. Faint. Faint as the idea of bliss. But steady. And I wanted to give it something it would have whether I was here or not, something to guide her, or him. Something true. A story.

And so in the moonlight I slipped out of bed, crept to my desk and flipped on Spunk.

"Long time, no see," he said. "Where you been?"

"Oh, questing."

"Yeah? Tell me about it."

"I will," I said, opening my web site. For the first time in ages I felt clearheaded, as if finally I knew less, but understood more. And I said, "Okay. Listen:

"Granted, I have been wildly medicated ....

end

Tom Grimes

is the author of the novels *A Stone of The Heart*, *Season's End*, and *City of God*, the plays *Spec* and *New World*, and the fiction anthology, *The Workshop: Seven Decades From The Iowa Writers Workshop*. His work has been named a *New York Times* Notable Book of the Year, a New & Noteworthy Paperback, and an Editor's Choice pick; it has won three Los Angeles Dramalogue Awards, been awarded a James Michener Fellowship, and has been selected for the Barnes & Noble Discover series. He now directs the MFA Program in Creative Writing at Southwest Texas State University.

Also available from Ludlow Press

Winner of the Ludlow Press Breakout Fiction Search Award!

"Retro '90s" East Village Romance

The setting of *The Losers' Club* is New York City. And it tells the story of Martin Sierra, an unlucky writer addicted to the personals. Early he encounters Nikki, his dream woman, who remains unattainable romantically, yet who becomes his friend and confidant during his comic misadventures. Set amid the vibrant bars and clubs of New York's East Village during the mid '90s, it is as much about a generation (we won't say "X") as it is about a specific time and place.

Ludlow Press
LudlowPress.Com
(order online:)

Advance praise for *The Losers' Club*:

Perez's is an exciting talent and his work goes far beyond most of what is published today."

—Henry Flesh,
Lambda Literary Award-winning author of *Michael* and *Massage*

"Funny, touching, and very much alive,
The Losers' Club throbs with the mid '90s subculture
of East Village night life.
Buoyant and highly entertaining—
I couldn't put it down."

—Stanley Cohen,
Angel Face

"Richard Perez's *The Losers' Club* moves fast without blurring, and documents New York City in all its self-invented variety: kitsch/retro bars and cafes, goth vampires, dyke rock bands, desperately clever personal ads, the endless cruise for a parking space, and loneliness so relentless its victims wind up feeling stillborn. In its quicksilver way, Perez's novel manages to be cheerful, bleak, and edgy all at once."

—John Vernon,
A Book of Reasons, Peter Doyle

"*The Losers' Club* gives a complete panoramic view
of the downtown New York scene of the '90s,
and along with all its flamboyant extremes...
this novel has an appealingly
old fashioned love story at its core."

—Madison Smartt Bell,
All Souls' Rising, Ten Indians

"Irrepressibly exuberant despite the pessimism and cynicism of youth, this first novel shows us a New York of the 1990's as vividly as Jay McInerney's BRIGHT LIGHTS, BIG CITY did the New York of the 1980s. Funny and heart-wrenching, THE LOSERS' CLUB is a winner."

—Ruth Doan MacDougall,
One Minus One, The Lilting House

"This is a story of youth, very well told, and it dwells in the mind long after a reader finishes it."

—Joanne Greenberg,
I Never Promised You a Rose Garden

"The prose in Richard Perez's first novel is charged with downtown energy. Edgy, mordant, sharply observed, *The Losers' Club* is funny and endearing-and wisely not so hip as to avoid a good grab for your heart."

—Marcie Hershman,
Safe in America, Tales of the Master Race

"Every generation must describe for itself what it means to be a young writer or artist struggling with anonymity and a mountain of rejection slips in a city like New York. Richard Perez's *The Losers' Club* tracks the poet Martin Sierra's melancholy and yet somehow humorous and hopeful life with an acid, yet not unsympathetic, pen. Perez has written a sharp, quick-paced satire of the personal ads subculture and the generally doomed semi-relationships it leads to, the bizarre and manic club life, where slam-dancing and other dangerous sports fail to mask the chronic—one might say terminal—loneliness of the participants. I especially like how the kaleidoscopic whirl of people and objects energizes the author and delights the reader with an almost photographic sense of time and place."

—Robert Siegel,
Best-selling author of *The Whalesong Trilogy*

"A fast, fun read."

—Richard Rhodes,
A Hole in the World, The Making of the Atomic Bomb
Pulitzer Prize Winner

"Rich Perez is a rare writer who moves with ease through the blasted lyric pain of childhood, the mysterious and sensuous and powerless world of being a kid, into the spotty drastic charm of '90s downtown flashy and downtrodden New York…having arrived at adulthood so that he can taste it with pleasure…."

—Eileen Myles,
Chelsea Girls, Cool For You

"Mr. Perez has written a kind of contemporary fable of his generation's life in Manhattan, a fable at once humorous and poignant."

—Alan Lelchuk,
Brooklyn Boy, American Mischief

"*The Losers' Club* is a fine novel. Richard Perez has a wonderful eye for details of the club scene and the humor to be found in urban decay. It is a book to be savored."

—Tim Sandlin,
Sorrow Floats, Social Blunders

"Richard Perez's *The Losers' Club* is a bittersweet trip through the East Village.... It's a tale of love lost and found among the coffee shops, mosh pits and art galleries. Take it from someone who's spent half a lifetime archiving the scene—this one's spot on!"

—Ron Kolm,
poet, author, member of the Unbearables

Welcome to the world of
The Losers' Club

{*ISBN:* 0-9713415-9-1   200 pages/*Fiction*}

Richard Perez will be your guide.

Read a free *Losers' Club* excerpt: "Up St. Marks Place" or "Madrecita" or
"CBGB"

@

LudlowPress.Com
(order online:)

Ludlow Press

HELLO MY NAME IS:

COST

Ludlow Press Books

For *individual* copies and info, log on:
LudlowPress.Com
or
write:
Ludlow Press
P.O. Box 2612
New York, NY 10009-9998

....

The Losers' Club
ISBN 0-9713415-9-1

WILL@epicqwest.com
ISBN 0-9713415-7-5

....

Distributed to the Trade by **Biblio** (a division of NBN)
To place an order and/or contact
Customer Service:
Phone (toll free): 1-800-462-6420
FAX (toll free): 1-800-338-4550
Email: custserv@nbnbooks.com